CHANGA'S SAFARI
VOLUME III

A NOVEL BY
MILTON J. DAVIS

Mvmedia

Fayetteville, Georgia

CHANGA'S SAFARI

VOLUME III

ISBN Number: 978-0-9960167-1-1

Cover art by Stanley Weaver, Jr.

Cover Design/Layout by URAEUS
Edited by Milton J. Davis

Manufactured in the United States of America

First Edition

AFRICA UNBOUND

By Charles R. Saunders

Changa Diop is an inimitable personage in the annals of sword-and-soul fiction: a fierce warrior, a shrewd merchant, and an intrepid sea-captain. And Changa's creator, Milton Davis, has envisioned a singular setting for his hero's magical and mercantile adventures: the Africa and Asia of the fifteenth century, an Old World milieu that combines legend and history in a way in which the line between the two blurs into invisibility, and the surroundings become mystical and intriguing.

In the previous two *Changa* volumes, the warrior-merchant – who is originally from the Kongo region but came of age in the cities of the East Coast of Africa – has journeyed not only through the rest of East Africa, but also across the Indian Ocean to such fabled places as India, China, Indonesia, and locations that cannot be found on medieval – or modern, for that matter – maps. He gains and loses fortunes and friends, and is haunted and hunted by a past that continually threatens to undo him.

Although Changa shares the same vulnerabilities as all humans, his indomitable strength of character always gives him a fighting change against the most formidable and insuperable of odds. Of course, it doesn't hurt that he is a master at the use of the unique throwing-knives that are the deadliest weapon of his native region.

In this third volume, Changa's business – and his fate – doesn't take him across the sea. He treks within Africa itself, a continent referred to as "dark" only by the ignorant. In fourteenth-century reality, however, Africa was festooned with cities and cultures that glittered like jewels. The names of the places to which Changa and his companions – especially his partner, a sorceress and healer named Panya – are drawn echo through a history that was long-lost, but is now being rediscovered:

Mombasa …

Sofala …

Kanem …

Bornu …

Oyo …

Songhai …

Nupe …

These are places that were as noteworthy during Changa's time as any location in Europe, Asia, or the Americas, and spoken of with a sense of awe and wonder.

Not only is Changa a compelling character; so is his setting. Between character and setting, Milton has crafted an amalgam of power and peril that defines the man – Changa – and the continent – Africa. This is Elder Africa, a land that shone brightly before the descent of the dark curtain of colonization and demoralization from which it continues to recover.

Now turn the page, and join Changa on his latest safari.

To Pop
Thanks for listening

Kitabu Cha Saba

(Book Seven)

Master of the Lake

The screams haunted him. It did not matter they came from the throats of thieves attempting to steal goats and grain, men some would say deserved their fate. Their desperate cries would soon join the melancholic cacophony of lamentations that echoed in his head every night. They would join those that had gone before them.

The cries subsided as the toxin took effect. The acrid smell of human waste cut through the humid air, forcing him to turn away and cover his nose. As the thieves fell still four stout women clothed in white cloth and beaded head wraps cut them free of their restraints then bound their naked bodies with long strips of cotton cloth, encasing them like a spider's feast. After wrapping them, the women poured a sweet smelling liquid over them from black calabashes. When the gourds were empty the women bowed to him, a look of relief on their faces. It was good fortune the thieves had come, otherwise one of the women or one of their family members would lie at his feet, wrapped and soaked in preparation for what was to come.

The porters entered moments later, four heavily muscled men wearing white loincloths, their faces hidden by wooden masks. They lifted the thieves from the floor then onto their broad shoulders like bags of sorghum. The thieves were still, their moving chests the only indication they were still alive. The porters carried them outside and he followed. The full moon shone like a mock sun, illuminating the grasses and lake with its pale light. The porters tied the thieves to donkeys then took them to as close to the lake shore as they dared. They untied their cargo, laid them on their backs, and then hurried away.

He did not leave. Each time he said he would not watch; each time he remained. Was it morbid fascination, or did he hope that it would not appear, that this would finally be done? He struggled for an answer as the lake water began to rise and fall like an inland tide. The surface roiled as fish fled to the surface, some so desperate as to seek refuge on the rocky shore. Mambas emerged, the huge reptiles fleeing into the nearby bush. He stood and then backed away as the lake calmed. It would not end. It would never end.

Thick, pale tentacles broke the lake's surface, illuminated by a sick green glow. They collapsed onto the lake shore then slithered around the encased bodies. The thieves barely responded as the tentacles contracted, still in the throes of the toxin. Then they slid away, dragging their offering with them. He prayed as they sank into the waters, hoping that this would be the last time, but he knew that would not be. The master of the lake must be fed. He waited until the bodies disappeared under the black waters, and then trudged back to the village.

1

FAMILIAR SHORES

The wind from the approaching storm piled the ocean into towering waves that crashed against the hulls of the fleeing dhows. Baharia clambered bare-footed across the decks and up the masts hoping to outrun the menacing maelstrom. Moving among them was a grim shirtless man whose broad shoulders and wide chest seemed as tense as his brown bearded face. He watched his crew hurry about then studied the encroaching dark clouds and black rain. They would make it to safe harbor, but not the harbor he wished.

Changa Diop wondered what he had done to deserve such circumstances. In a matter of months he'd witnessed the death of a dear friend, the disappearance of another he considered a brother and the departure of a man who was like an uncle to him. Though the crew around him was the best these angry seas knew, the losses cut deep. His only comfort was that amongst it all he'd come to love a woman whose beauty was second only to her strength. That woman approached him through the smattering rain, a look of concern on her face.

"There is nothing I can do," Panya said, her tone apologetic. "Sometimes Oya must have her way."

Changa placed a gentle hand on her shoulder. "So be it. It's not like we've haven't weathered storms before."

"So why are you so concerned?" Panya asked.

"The dhows will definitely suffer damage," he replied. "This means we'll have to seek port sooner than I wished."

"Mombasa," Panya said.

Changa nodded.

"Maybe it won't be so bad," she said. "It's been years since we left."

Changa answered her with a skeptical gaze. He shrugged then headed to the helm. Nafasi, Mikaili's former apprentice now the new navigator, struggled with the wheel as he shouted orders over the howling wind. Mikaili trained the young Swahili well, but Changa still couldn't help thinking they would have been far beyond the storm's grasp if his old friend learned hands gripped the wheel.

Nafasi's expression mirrored Changa's thoughts.

"I'm sorry, bwana," he said. "It seems we will not beat the storm."

"Have the men secure the decks," Changa said. "We'll take our blows then heal in Mombasa."

Nafasi relayed Changa's orders to the crew then drummed them to the other dhows. Moment later the storm overtook them with unexpected fury. Changa struggled on deck with the strongest of his crew, fighting to keep his dhow intact and his men on board. The wind's rage increased, tearing at the sails and rocking the Kazuri like a twig in a swift stream.

"Get those sails down!" Changa shouted. The baharia were clambering across the slick deck to obey his command when the dhow lurched, throwing everyone off their feet. Changa slid across the deck then slammed hard against the bulwark.

"Bwana Diop!" Nafasi's yell cut through the howling wind. Changa looked to see his young navigator gesturing frantically to the opposite bulwark. Changa's eyes followed Nafasi's finger; the sight that incited fear in the man sparked resignation in Changa.

A pair of massive gnarled hands gripped the opposite side. Changa grasped the bulwark rim against his back then pulled up to his feet. He took a hard look at the men forming around him. There was fear in their eyes but their hands sought the swords at their sides. They were Kazuri baharia; they would face whatever heaved onto the ship. But Changa knew their efforts would be fruitless.

"Get everyone below," he said. "Now!"

Nafasi rounded up the baharia then led them away. Changa unfastened the throwing knives attached to his waist belt, weapons forged from the iron of his homeland. They were the only arms that could kill the creature rising over the rail.

The beast collapsed onto the deck with a thud that shook the wood beneath Changa's feet. It stood twice Changa's height on thick legs punctuated by wide webbed feet. Slick grey skin stretched over its bulging muscles, its cold eyes wide and unblinking. Its face resembled that of a great fish, the wide mouth opening and closing in time with the gill slits on its thick neck. Long muscled arms hung where fins should be, its clawed hands almost scraping the deck. Despite its frightening visage Changa did not hesitate in his attack; this was an old foe he would never be rid of until the day he returned to his homeland of Kongo.

The tebo lumbered toward him, raising its massive arms over its thick head. Changa continued his headlong assault until the creature brought its arms down to strike. He darted to the left and the tebo's fists slammed into the deck, sending wood splitters in every direction. The floorboards shuddered and Changa stumbled; the deep cut he hoped to deliver to the beast's torso became only a minor scratch. The tebo twisted, swinging its right arm at Changa's head. Changa ducked the clumsy swipe then stepped close to the beast, slashing upward with both knives. The tebo's thick skin opened from its midsection to its neck. A putrid smell hit Changa almost like a blow; he stumbled away then was struck by the beast's left claw.

His knives flew from his hands as he flipped head over feet from the powerful blow. The bulwark prevented him from flying into the ocean, but such luck was short lived. The tebo wrapped its arms around him before he could recover then carried Changa over the bulwark and into the churning sea. They plunged into the water, sinking under the surface like a living anchor. Changa struggled to hold his breath as he pounded on the beast's shoulder and head. The tebo's grasp tightened as they descended deeper into the darkening ocean. Changa kept striking the beast though his blows seemed useless. Only the iron of Kongo could kill the beast and his knives were far from his weakening hands. With the last of his breath escaping him Changa swept his eyes over the beast and found what he searched for. The tebo's gills fluttered on both sides of its thick neck, sifting life giving oxygen from the water. With the last his strength Changa plunged his hands into the organs. The tebo shuddered then tightened its grip, no longer content to let the waters claim Changa's life. Changa gripped the gills' innards then ripped them away. The tebo flung Changa away, its small mouth forming a pain induced oval as it clawed at its damaged neck. Changa swam for the surface, fighting against the instinct to open his mouth and inhale. His head cleared the surface just as he lost his battle, the salt tinged air the sweetest he'd ever inhaled.

Instead of the swirling waves of a stormy sea he was surrounded by calm blackness. Above him dark clouds still held sway; unleashing bolts of lightning that lit the otherwise dim surroundings. No rain splattered his head and no wind pushed him about. It was if he was held in a dome of glass protected from the storm's fury. A knowing smile came to his face.

"Oya's daughter," he said.

His hands burned. Deep cuts crisscrossed his palms and fingers where he held the tebo's gills. The briny water caused them to sting, but Changa was used to dealing with such pain. Stranded in the ocean surrounded by churning seas, he had no choice but to suffer silently until help arrived.

A familiar bow breached his bubble of solitude. The Kazuri sped toward him, chasing away the calm protecting him from the storm. Rain pattered against his head.

"There he is!" he heard Panya shout.

The Kazuri veered away from him. Baharia lined its bulwark, as rope flew from their hands. Changa grabbed the closest then gritted his teeth as he pulled himself up the side. The baharia grabbed him as soon as they could reach him and hauled him over the bulwark like a prized fish.

He tumbled onto his back. Panya was on him immediately, covering his face with kisses.

"From one drowning to another," he managed to say.

Nafasi loomed over her shoulder, a satisfied grin on his face.

"Welcome back, nahoda. You chose a strange time to go for a swim."

His words rang of Mikaili, which made Changa smile even broader.

"My friend insisted," Changa said. "Unfortunately he was not a good swimmer."

"Can you walk?" Panya asked.

"I think so," he said.

Changa stood and his men cheered. The storm waned, but the winds still blew strong and the rain still fell.

"Everyone back to work!" Nafasi shouted. "This storm is not through with us!"

Panya gestured to Changa and he followed her below deck to her cabin. He sat on her bunk as she rummaged through her shelves and concoctions for the right combination of salves and herbs to heal his wounds. Changa grinned as she flittered about. She was still taking care of him, healing his body and spirit from the constant onslaught of Usenge. Despite the experience, wisdom and the talisman he'd gathered throughout his journeys Panya was the true reason for his endurance. It was good to have the uncertainty lifted between them and to enjoy her love full and uninhibited.

She turned suddenly, a green urn clutched in her right hand and a thin bottle of a clear liquid in the other.

"This should do it," she said. Her smiled faded and her eyes went wide.

"Changa, your hands!"

Changa looked at his hands. They'd swollen to twice their normal size, the blood oozing from them the color of the tebo's ichor.

"What is this?" he managed to say before pain bolted up his arms then struck his head like a hammer. He blacked out.

"You continue to live. You are persistent, I must admit."

Changa opened his eyes to blackness. He groped about, feeling his nude body but nothing else. He tried to stand but the shadows held him in place better than any chain. A faint light appeared before him, resembling the sun rising over a distant horizon. The light rose for a moment then meandered toward him, growing brighter as it approached. After what seemed like ages the light hovered before him. Changa's senses were overwhelmed with a familiar stench.

"Usenge," he spat.

The viscous laugh flowed around him like pus.

"So this is where I slay you?" Changa said.

There was no laughter this time, only a sensation of anger that made Changa smile.

"You dream, son of Mfumu," Usenge replied. "Your blood is thin like an old man. You will die at my hands like your father if you continue this farce."

Changa's invisible smile grew wider. "You speak as if I have a choice, ndoki. Every step I've taken from the day I left Kongo was to bring me back home. I will return, and I will kill you."

"Forget your promise. It is beyond your powers to fulfill. Stay in Sofala and marry your Yoruba woman. Do so, and my tebo will bother you no more.

Changa's smile seemed to ease the darkness. "I sense fear in you, Usenge. Nothing you say can keep me from returning home."

"The man speaks, but how does the boy who saw his father slain feel?"

Images coalesced about Changa, visions of that fateful day. Thandeka, his mother's personal servant, held his face between her calloused hands, forcing him to view his father's execution. Usenge gripped the execution sword in his bloody hands, his true face obscured by his hideous war mask. Behind the usurper Changa's mother and sisters wept, flanked by Usenge's warriors. Fear and anger rushed through Changa, but it was the fear that took root, a fear sparked by an eight year old boy who thought he might be discovered and killed as well. But that fear was replace by a deeper emotion, one placed in his breast by the eyes of his father the moment before the sword fell on his neck. Somehow the kabaka found his hidden son among the crowd of mourning subjects, instilling in him the words forming the foundation of Changa's efforts.

"Avenge me."

Changa felt the mood shift about him, the darkness giving way to growing luminance.

"Your woman saves you again, boy," Usenge spoke. "She cannot do so forever."

Brightness doused Changa, blinding him. He shaded his eyes then saw Panya hovering over him, relief ruling her smiling face. He tried to sit up but she pushed him back down.

"You came back to me," she said. Baharia crowded into the cabin; Nafasi grinned as he peered over Panya's shoulder.

"Our nahoda tricks death again! Praise Allah!" he announced.

The men repeated his words, each of them reaching out to touch Changa before returning to the deck.

"What happened?" he asked Panya.

Panya placed a damp rag on his forehead. "The tebo's blood contained venom. It was venom I had no cure for."

"So you did not save me?"

The relief in Panya's eyes deepened. "Not with my medicines. I prayed to Oya and the men prayed to Allah."

Changa sat up, ignoring Panya's attempt to press him back down.

"Usenge grows stronger," Changa said. "But so do I. I must finish this soon."

Panya didn't reply. She stared at him for a moment then looked away.

"What do you wish to say?" he asked.

"Must it be finished? Must you return?"

"I saw him, Panya. I felt his fear. He's fighting me with his nyama and it is not working. I was stronger this time against the tebo. I have been the last few times, ever since I returned from the Middle Kingdom. He knows he cannot defeat me with his power, so now he tries to weaken me with fear."

"Can you truly defeat him, Changa?" Panya asked. Changa grasped Panya's shoulders with his hands. "What is this? Do you not believe I can do this?"

"You almost died, Changa, and I could not help you. Nothing I did could stop the poison's work. I prayed to Oya and still I felt helpless. It took me a long time to love you, Bakonga. I don't wish to lose you so soon."

Changa chuckled then pulled Panya into a gentle embrace.

"Don't you see? His nyama wanes against me. Mine is stronger, and now I have what I need to raise an army to return home. Most of all, I have you."

"Still," she said as she pressed her cheek into his chest, "I worry for you."

Changa gently grasped her chin, lifting her lips into a passionate kiss.

"I can't believe you said that. As much as we've been through together?"

"Changa Diop, you are many things, but you are not immortal." Changa kissed her again. "Well, until I'm dead I'll believe otherwise."

2

SETTLING SCORES

Changa's fleet survived the storm but not without substantial damage. There was no choice; they would have to moor in Mombasa before continuing to Sofala. Changa was on deck when the white stone warehouses lining the Mombasa landing came into view. They entered the harbor with the rising sun, a gentle warm breeze pushing them to safe mooring. It was a bittersweet sight. Before him was the city where he learned the merchant trade and mastered the dhow, where a kind man took it upon himself to train him. Here also was the city where he almost lost his life to the machinations of that same man's sons if not for the Tuareg's alertness and Panya's skill. He looked over his left shoulder, almost expecting to see his silent brother standing beside him. Instead he saw Nafasi approaching.

"Bwana, what you wish to do?" the young navigator asked.

"How is the mood of the men?" Changa asked.

Nafasi grinned. "Excited and anxious. Mombasa is home for many of them."

"I have a few friends here myself. We'll anchor as close as we need but not too close. Let them go ashore in shifts and caution them to be wary."

"Will we trade here?"

Changa shook his head. "A little. The men can do what they wish, but the bulk of our cargo remains intact. Sofala is our destination."

"Yes, bwana," Nafasi turned to walk away.

"Nafasi!" Changa said.

The young navigator turned. "Yes, bwana?"

"Enough with this bwana stuff. You are a man of rank among us and most of all, you are my friend. Changa will do fine."

Nafasi grinned like a satisfied simba. "Yes, bwana…I mean Changa!"

Panya joined him soon afterwards.

"So what are our plans?"

"We'll stay long enough to effect repairs then we're off to Sofala."

"You're not going to call on Yusef?"

A broad smile came to his face. "That would be impolite, wouldn't it?"

"Yes it would. Besides, it would be good for your spirits. The best friends are the old ones."

"I can't go ashore without doing a little trading," Changa commented.

"Then do it. Don't confine yourself because of recent grief."

Moments later Changa rowed with a contingent of Kazuri baharia toward the Mombasa shore. Despite the threat of discovery by Belay's sons Changa was in high spirits. Panya's suggestion that he visit Yusef was an excellent idea. It had been a long time since he'd seen his old friend and it would be good to see him again.

But first there was a bit of trading to do. Changa and his men carried their goods directly to the warehouse district; their arms wrapped around urns filled treasures from the East. He hoped to do some discreet trading for items to repair the ships and foodstuffs, but the word of his rare objects swept the docks like a dry season fire. Soon he and his men were surrounded by haggling Swahili anxious for porcelain plates to mount in their walls and jade statues to decorate their pedestals. Changa reveled in the attention; the more buyers, the higher the price.

"Eighty dinars?!?" the buyer exclaimed, a small man with a surprisingly loud voice. The other traders stared at Changa with consternation and disbelief. The price for the porcelain plate in Changa's hand was apparently much more than they were will to pay...for now.

"That is the price, my brother," Changa said. "This is porcelain from the heart of the Middle Kingdom itself, not a cheap imitation that usually finds its way to our shores."

Changa held up the plate, its surface decorated in blue images depicting life scenes of the far away land. He placed his hand behind it; the image of his hand appeared as a shadow through the plate.

"Thin enough to see through but tough like nails." He slammed the plate against the selling table. Everyone reared back expecting to be showered with shards. Instead the plate remained intact in Changa's hand.

"It's worth every penny," he said. "My brother, I would not cheat anyone. My father raised me to be an honest man."

Naragisi ibn Belay stepped from the throng, flanked by his brothers Niko and Jengo. Changa's good mood faded as his first instinct was to grab his throwing knives. But he promised himself and Panya he would do no harm while in Mombasa. Besides, he'd left his knives aboard the Kazuri.

"Greetings, brothers," he said instead. "I see Allah has kept you well."

"And you," Naragisi replied. As the elder brother he always spoke for the three when they were together.

The three of them perused the table with calculating eyes. Changa watched them, curious about what direction the conversation would turn.

"It seems you have done well on your safari to the East," Naragisi said. "Our father would be proud."

The statement almost made Changa curse. The trio was a

constant disappointment to Belay, so much so that on his death
bed the respected merchant astonished everyone by bequeathing
the bulk of his worth to Changa.

"Yes, I think he would have," Changa said.

Jengo stepped forward, picking up a particularly fine
porcelain plate.

"Yes, you have done well indeed. It is fortuitous that we
loaned you the use of our dhows."

"I use that which was given to me," Changa said.

"Though for my brothers I will give a special price for
anything you see here."

Jengo's eyes narrowed. He pointed at Changa as he was
known to do when angered.

"You play a dangerous game, mhadimu!"

"Be quiet, Jengo!" Naragisi said.

Changa grinned at them both. Such insults had long lost
their sting.

"We're glad to see such prosperity touch our brother.
If you were Swahili you would hold a high position among us.
But things being as they are…" Naragisi flashed his infamous
predatory smile.

"Thank you for your well wishes…brother," Changa said.
"If there is nothing else, I have work to do."

The brothers ogled the table a moment more then nodded
to Changa.

"Allah be with you," Naragisi said.

"And with you," Changa replied.

Changa frowned. A polite Naragisi was a dangerous thing.
Retaliation was in process. In what form it would come he wasn't
certain.

A group of boys played nearby, their raucous activity
competing with the haggling at the table. Changa turned over
the selling to his men. He sauntered to the boys, reached into his
money pouch then took out a shiny gold piece.

"Who wants to earn a piece of gold?" he shouted.

The boys broke away from their game then crowded around Changa like a flock of hungry fowl, their hands reaching for his gold piece. Changa lifted the coin over his head, well out of reach of the eager boys.

"Who knows of Yusef the ivory trader?" he asked.

"I do! I do!" they all shouted.

Changa grinned, expecting the unanimous response.

"Where does he live?" Changa asked.

"In Stone Town!" they replied.

"No!" one boy shouted. "He lives in the country town. Yusef hates the Swahili!"

Changa found the speaker of those true words standing away from the throng of excited boys, his arms folded across his narrow chest.

"Come here, boy," he gestured. He went into his pouch again, giving silver coins to the boys then chasing them away.

The boy with the correct answer sauntered up to Changa, a suspecting look in his young eyes.

"What's your name?" Changa asked.

"Taka," the boy replied.

Changa gave Taka the gold piece. "Go to Yusef and tell him Changa Diop is here. I'll give you another gold piece when you return and a third gold piece if you return today."

"Bwana Yusef is a big slow man," Taka said. "He trudges like the tembos he hunts."

Changa laughed. Taka truly knew Yusef.

"A tembo can be swifter than the fastest man when there is a purpose. Now go. You're wasting time."

The boy grinned then ran off into the crowd.

Changa turned his attention back to trading. The transactions were swift and the business very encouraging. They quickly collected the supplies needed to repair the ships then hired porters on the spot to carry them to the shore. By the time they reached the beach darkness settled on Mombasa, the call for evening prayer echoing across the city.

"We'll stay ashore overnight," Changa told his men. "In the morning we'll begin repairs then be on our way. If any of you wish to be with family go and do so, otherwise I'll pay for lodging."

He distributed a share of the profits to his men.

"We did well today my brothers. Imagine what waits for us in Sofala!"

*   *   *

Despite the late hour the Belay compound was well lit. Lanterns hung on the walls surrounding veranda, providing light for Naragisi's servants as they set up their cots for the night. Inside, the sons of Belay gathered around a circular table, cups of Axumite coffee giving off rich aromas.

"It's an insult he's still alive!" Jengo said.

"His very presence disgraces us!" Niko added. "What was baba thinking?"

"He was thinking of his lazy sons who squandered his hard earned wealth and a mhadimu who took advantage of his weakness," Naragisi said.

"There is no need to insult us," Jengo said.

"Yes there is." Naragisi stood and walked away from the table, a look of disgust on his face.

"If it wasn't for your indolence Changa Diop would be nothing," he said.

"You blame us?" Niko said. "We didn't go to Mogadishu and bring him back!"

"No you didn't, but if you had shown any effort toward learning the merchant trade instead of clinging to mama's kanga and wailing like goats he would have never thought of teaching that bastard the trade."

"What about you, Naragisi?" Jengo said. "You had no hand in this? What are you, the perfect son? You are the eldest. Why did baba pass his inheritance to Changa over you? It seems to me baba had three reasons not to give us his inheritance; you were the first and most disappointing one."

Naragisi didn't reply, for Jengo's statement was true. All his life he'd challenged his father's authority and refused to take his advice. Instead of learning the trade he took to the coast, using his wealth to build a plantation to supply crops to the stone town. Without Naragisi to pass on his knowledge Belay turned to Jengo and Niko who were obviously not interested in doing any work of any kind. But there was Changa Diop, a man whose natural curiosity vaulted him from a valued bodyguard to a surrogate son. For this they were ridiculed throughout Stone Town.

"The reasons are not important now,' Naragisi said.

"What is important is what we do about it. How to we settle the score?"

"Mercenaries?" Jengo suggested.

Naragisi shook his head. "Too expensive and too unreliable."

"Boycott the sale of his goods?" Niko said.

Naragisi shook his head again. "He has no intentions of selling the bulk of his goods here. We're just a way stop to Sofala. He'll trade along the coast until he gets to Sofala…unless he has nothing to trade!"

Jengo and Niko looked at their brother's elated expression with puzzlement.

"And how do we cause that to happen?" Jengo asked.

"By combining your suggestions," Naragisi answered.

The elder Belay nodded to his brothers. "I must be off.

This will take some time and some gold. You both will pay your share."

"Pay?" Niko exclaimed. "Pay for what? I'm not giving up one drachma until I know what I'm paying for!"

Naragisi smiled like a hyena before a kill. "Believe me brother, once I'm done you'll be tempted to give me everything you own. But of course you won't."

*   *   *

Changa and Panya spent the night on the deck of the Kazuri making love under the starry sky. Though the threat of tebos was ever-present and his enemies only a few oar strokes away, Changa felt no fear. It seemed whatever enmity caused by his action had either died or subsided. The lone exception was Belay's sons, but that was to be expected. It's easier to keep an eye on one enemy instead of many and Changa was making sure he had many eyes.

Panya stirred and he hugged her tight.

"You were like the storm," she whispered.

"And you were Oya," he replied.

She laughed as she sat up and began dressing. "Come, the men will be on deck soon."

"As if they weren't earlier?"

Panya's eyes went wide. "They wouldn't!"

"Of course they would. They're baharia."

Panya stood over him and shook an accusing finger.

"Never again, Changa. Never again!"

Changa folded his hands behind his head and grinned.

"I'm sorry, Panya. I was caught up in the moment. I didn't hear you complaining."

A smile came to her face despite her struggle to prevent it.

"I hate you sometimes."

Changa winked. "Liar."

She kicked his leg then turned and sauntered away. Changa watched her swaying hips and relived the night in his mind.

The morning brought his cohorts to the deck eager to go into town and spend their new found wealth. Nafasi organized the shore parties in shifts so the ships were constantly attended for repairs and to handle any additional merchants seeking to trade. Changa went down to his cabin, tallying the previous day's profits. If the trend of exchange continued he would be a very rich man indeed. He was entering the totals in his ledger when there was a knock on the wall.

Nafasi stood outside the cabin.

"Bwana…I mean Changa, there is someone from Stone Town to see you."

Taka jumped before Naragisi draped in new clothes. Nafasi grabbed a handful of his shirt then lifted him onto his toes.

"No one introduced you yet, boy!" Naragisi fussed.

"It's okay, Nafasi. Let him go."

Nafasi dropped the boy to his feet. The boy straightened his clothes as he glared at the navigator.

"So Taka my friend, you found Yusef?"

Taka nodded then held out his hand for the coin Changa promised. Changa rubbed his chin instead.

"How do I know you're not lying to me?"

Taka grinned "You don't. Bwana Yusef told me it has been a long time since he'd seen you, Kibwana."

Nafasi grabbed the boy again. "Watch your insults!"

Changa laughed. "No, Naragisi, everything is fine. Kibwana is what Yusef calls me."

Nafasi looked surprised. "You allow this?"

"When you see Yusef you'll understand."

Taka pulled away then shook his extended hand.

"Not yet," Changa said. "When I see my friend you'll get paid."

Changa and the others loaded a boat with gifts then set out for shore. They followed Taka through Stone Town then to the bridge that linked the Swahili stronghold to Country Town. Changa always preferred Country Town to Stone Town. The strict hierarchy of the Swahili didn't apply to the mainland city. It was a place where the culture or lineage of a person did not matter. It made sense that Yusef would reside on the mainland instead of the islands. Yusef was Swahili but he was never one to follow rules, especially when it came to indulging in alcohol. It was his only weakness and the main reason why much of Changa's time spent with the big man became situations where sharp wit and a sharp sword were essential. But besides his crew Changa couldn't ask for a better friend.

Yusef's home wasn't difficult to find. The large coral brick house was situated at the edge of the town, an exact replica of the homes the Swahili cherished. A stone house was not only a sturdy home built to resist the vagrancies of coastal weather; it was a symbol of the owners' status and wealth.

"Yusef's fortunes have apparently improved," Panya commented.

"It seems so," Changa said. "Tembo hunting seems to suit him."

They were almost to the beautifully carved door when it swung open. Yusef ibn Abdalla stepped through the opening, a wide smile on his bearded face, his arms stretched out wide.

"Kibwana! Panya! Welcome! Welcome! Welcome!"

He rushed them, wrapping them in his massive arms. The slight smell of wine wafted from his grinning visage and Changa smiled. Some things never change.

"Let them go!" a forceful female voice ordered. "You'll kill them before we get a chance to entertain them."

Kenja emerged from the house, her diminutive frame a contrast to Yusef's bulk. What she lacked in stature she more than made up for in beauty and personality. Changa remembered when they first met her during their encounter with Mwanamke Tembo and her sister, Shange. She was a woman who wouldn't be denied and Yusef fell for her like a bush deer to a well thrown spear. She carried the product of their marriage, a baby girl that stared at Changa and Panya with playful eyes.

"Welcome, Changa," Kenja stood on her tiptoes and kissed Changa's cheek. She went to Panya and bowed.

"Sister, come inside with me. We will talk of important things while these two lie to each other."

Panya laughed. "Let's do so. I've brought you a few things from China."

Kenja's eyes brightened. "See fahali? You should bring more gifts home to me."

"I bring you food. That should be enough."

Kenja swatted Yusef's butt. "I should take my children and run to the bush. You don't love me."

Yusef scooped Kenja and the baby into his arms. Kenja smiled despite trying her best to remain cross.

"Then I would cry like a little tembo until you returned."

"Put me down and go play with your friend. Panya and I have women things to discuss."

Yusef placed Kenja down gently then she and Panya went into the house. A chorus of voices greeted them.

"How many children does that make now?" Changa asked.

"Eight. Four of them are mine." Yusef placed his hands on his waist and struck a proud stance.

"Allah has been good to you," Changa said.

"And to you," Yusef replied.

They strolled to a large acacia tree in the center of the courtyard then sat on the wicker stools beneath the branches.

"It's very good to see you, Kibwana. For a time I thought the sea had taken you."

"I'm too mean for that," Changa replied. "We have returned, at least some of us have."

Yusef took on a solemn face. "There are three who are not with you. I hoped they were in the harbor with your dhows."

Changa sighed. "Zakee is dead. We lost the Tuareg in Ethiopia, and Mikaili finally decided to heed his calling into the priesthood."

"So two dead and one gone home." Yusef shook his head.

"One dead for sure, the other is not certain." Changa still held out hope for his silent friend although he knew Yusef's words were most likely true.

He decided to change the subject.

"So what of you? It seems the ivory trade has done well for you."

Yusef pushed out his chest again. "It would be correct to say that I am a wealthy man. The demand for ivory is strong and the tembos are abundant in the interior. But the more the demand the less ivory I need."

"Kenja is a blessing in more ways than one," Changa said with a wink.

"I think I had something to do with it," Yusef pouted.

"I know you, Yusef. I'm sure Kenja has nine children."

They laughed as a servant brought them tea.

"You will stay the night?" Yusef asked.

"Of course." Changa sipped his tea and was officially home.

"Excellent. We'll prepare a fabulous feast. You will always remember the day you came to visit me, Kibwana!"

Changa's travels exposed him to all types of luxuries; the village feast in the Middle Kingdom after his return from Kara Korim and the raja's dinner in Vijayanagar among the best. But Yusef's dinner rivaled both because it was so familiar. The four of them sat before a low table atop a woven mat, the children sitting before a smaller table near the adults. Changa broke off a piece ugali, rolling it into a tight ball before dipping it into the steaming rice, smiling as the spicy mix burned a path down his throat. There was cabbage, cassava, banana and goat stew, and Kenja's special meal, duck cooked in coconut milk. Changa and Panya sat side by side as did Yusef and Kenja, the children's laughter bringing brightness to the occasion. Changa's men gathered close by, enjoying the succulent meal from bowls while boasting and teasing. As they feasted the servants carried a large gourd to the table, and then sat in it in the center.

"Now what is this?" Yusef exclaimed. "It seems my wife has planned a special surprise!"

Kenja looked puzzled. "I didn't prepare this, nor did I have it ordered. It's a mystery to me as well."

Changa became suspicious. "Where did this come from?"

"The porters who brought it said you were expecting it," the servant said. "It is a gift from your brothers."

Changa jumped to his feet. "Everyone get away from the table now!"

He drew his shimsar as the gourd began shaking. Yusef swept up Kenja and the children.

"Get them inside!" he shouted.

Kenja did not argue, shooing the children before her. Changa's men were on their feet as well, their blades in their hands as the gourd cracked open. A writhing mass of black mambas spilled onto the table, slithering in every direction. Changa grabbed Panya's arm as he stumbled back.

"Naragisi is behind this," Changa growled as he hacked at the snakes. "This is only the beginning."
Together they killed the serpents.

"The dhows?" she said.

"They are probably under attack. Take half the men and go inside. I think we'll have visitors soon, Samburu most likely."

"I will stay with you," Panya said.

"No. You are my second in command. You will protect

those inside if the Samburu get by us."

Panya stared at Changa for a moment then ran to the house, yelling the names of the baharia chosen. The rattle of shields and assegais caught Changa's attention, his head snapping to the direction of Yusef's gate. The elaborately carved gates crashed to the ground and Samburu warriors poured in.

"Naragisi," Changa whispered. He reached for his knife bag before realizing he'd left it in the Kazuri.

"Baharia!" he shouted. His remaining dhow mates ran to him and they met the Samburu in the middle of the courtyard with sabers and swords. Changa twisted sideways, avoiding the thrown assegai meant for his chest. He twisted again; dodging the spear thrust for his gut then slicing his attacker's hand from his arm. The man had no time to cry out for Changa's shimsar found his neck first. A shield slammed against him knocking him sideways; he instinctively pulled his foot away, avoiding the stab from the pointed end of the cow skin safeguard. Changa caught the spear thrust with his free hand, wrenching it from his opponent's hand then stabbed the Samburu's foot with it. The man howled and dropped his shield. Changa stabbed him again, this time in the chest. He let go of the assegai as the man fell away.

A group of Samburu broke away, heading for the house.

"No you don't!" Yusef bellowed before running after them.

Changa glanced around him. The Samburu dwindled, the baharia chopping them down with practiced precision.

Changa ran toward his friend but his path was suddenly blocked by a towering Samburu. This man held no shield or assegai like his brothers. Instead he wielded two swords, a curving slashing blade and a short stabbing sword. Changa recognized him as Naragisi's henchman, Leleruk.

"It seems this will be a day of settling scores," he said to the Samburu.

Leleruk grinned. "It seems so."

Leleruk attacked with ferocious swiftness. Each blow hammered Changa's sword, each thrust tested the Bakonga's agility. Changa sweated, thinking for a moment this was a possessed man before him, so relentless was his attack. He kept the pace and his strength did not falter. It was obvious why Naragisi chose Leleruk as his assassin, for his skills were more than formidable. He was a man Changa would have selected, a man whose skills rivaled the Tuareg's. The thought of his old friend fueled him. It was time to end this duel.

Changa slammed his foot into the brute's shin. Leleruk stumbled back, dropping his left sword hand instinctively. Changa pounced, blocking the curve blade meant for his neck as he slammed his fist into the man's jaw. The stabbing blade fell from the Samburu's hand; Changa let his momentum twist him around as he crouched low then swept Leleruk off his feet. The man crashed onto his back, his other blade flying from his hand. Changa scooped up the Samburu's thrusting sword and drove it through the man, pinning him to the ground. He jumped over the body and ran to Yusef's house, barely noticing the Samburu's dying scowl.

The house echoed with the sounds of struggle. Yusef yelled and cursed, swinging back and forth with his scimitar. The Samburu in the rear held their ground against his powerful but unskilled assault; the Samburu vanguard was held in check by Panya and the baharia's resistance. Kenja guarded her children, a sword in her small hands and the look of a determined mother on her face. The children cowered behind Kenja, their cries reaching Changa's ears as he joined the fray.

"Left!" he shouted. Yusef immediately stepped to his left, allowing Changa through. He smashed his shoulder into the Samburu's shield before him, knocking the man off his feet and into his cohorts. Carnage ensued as Changa's speed and skill, backed by Yusef's potent fury, descended on the Samburu like a towering wave. The other Samburu were suddenly trapped between Changa and Yusef's onslaught and Panya, Kenja and baharia rage. The Samburu could have fled the hopeless scenario, but they were true warriors. They fought to the last man.

Changa and the others found no joy in their victory. The fight was far from over.

"The dhows are surely under attack," he said, his eyes locked on Panya.

"There is no way we'll get back in time," she answered.

"There is one way," Yusef said. "Come quickly!"

Yusef led them to a large structure behind his house. He opened the gate, went inside then emerged with two saddled stallions. Panya and Changa mounted quickly.

"Ride fast, Kibwana," Yusef said. "I hope you arrive in time."

Panya and Changa galloped through the dark streets of Country Town then across the bridge into Stone Town. The way was easier to decipher once they reached the Swahili town because of the torch lit streets. As the docks came into view a wavering light rose over the dark horizon. The dread Changa felt since the attack at Yusef's home coalesced into terror. The Hazina and Sendibada burned in the far harbor; the Kazuri was beginning to ignite. Flaming arrows arched through the dark sky from the beach, streaking toward the three dhows.

Changa and Panya kicked their horses hard and the mounts ran onto the beach. The archers were so consumed with their nefarious task that they never saw the horse carrying the hulking warrior with the raised sword until it was too late. Changa killed them all in moments, their burning arrows extinguished in the wet sand and surf.

He dismounted then ran up shore to a group of fishing boats. Panya was beside him in moments and they climbed into the nearest vessel together. Their strokes were determined and sure despite their fatigue. The dhows came into closer view and the horror revealed. The Sendibada and Hazina were fully engulfed in flame. Baharia jumped for their lives, rescued by their brethren in boats similar to Changa's. The Kazuri burned as well but the crew fought furiously against the flames. Other boats sped to the surviving dhow to join the fight. No sooner had Changa's boat reach the Kazuri did a rope tumble over the side to them. They clambered up and climbed over the bulwark to the dying inferno.

Nafasi met Changa, his soot covered face streaked with tears.

"Forgive me, Changa. Forgive me!"

Changa held his despair in check as he patted the man's shoulder.

"You did your best I'm sure. Let's get this fire out and check on our brothers."

Another hour of frantic work finally doused the flames. Panya moved among the exhausted men, checking them for burns and other injuries. Changa walked among them as well, sharing encouraging words. He refused to look toward the fires still blazing in his periphery. His dhows and his future were being consumed, years of work and sacrifice destroyed in one careless night. Looking in his comrades faces was more painful. They trusted him, following him to the East and back, battling foes of all kinds and risking their own lives for a dream that was not theirs. Now their hopes were going up in flames, soon to rest on the bottom of Mombasa harbor. True, there were goods in the belly of the Kazuri but the real wealth was contained in the larger dhows. They were ruined.

The men gathered around him after the fire died. Together they watched the Sendibada and Hazina burn then sink into the blue waters. The Sendibada sank first during the night; the sun peeked over the horizon as the Hazina's mast disappeared under the waves.

Changa's hands tightened on the bulwark. His grieving

was done. He turned to his men, his face stern. They managed to rescue the crew of both ships, so the Kazuri's deck held little room. He looked into the face of each one of them and saw his resolve reflected in their expressions. They were ready to act.

"So here we are again," he said. "The Fates must love us, for they are always challenging our will."
Smiles and head nods rippled through the crowd. Panya grinned, her eyes encouraging.

"I will not lie to you. We have lost almost everything this night. But I promise that you will not go home empty handed. I know who is responsible for this and if you trust me one more time I'll make sure they pay. There is no way we can recover all that was lost, but when this is done you will have something to justify your years away from your loved ones. This I assure you."

Changa folded his arms across his chest. "Those of you who are well enough get your swords and follow me."

Half of the men scrambled away to do as ordered. Panya came to his side.

"You're going after Belay's sons," she said.
Changa nodded.
"They will be waiting for us."
"I know. Allah have mercy on their souls. I won't."

Changa, Panya and his men climbed down the Kazuri's hull, filling the waiting boats. They rowed to a beach crowded with onlookers who had apparently gathered during the night to watch the death of his dhows. They waded ashore, pushing through the excited crowd. Changa led them through the narrow streets to Warehouse Road. They wound through the maze of roads and alleys until they came to Belay's warehouse. The building was guarded as expected by a collection of various armed men, some Swahili, some from Country Town, but all lacking the martial experience of Changa and his seasoned baharia. They broke and fled as soon as Changa advanced, leaving the warehouse open.

"Nafasi, go inside and take inventory. Once you have an

accurate count, station men outside the door. No one is to enter. This is our warehouse now."

"Yes, Changa." Nafasi hurried to implement Changa's plan.

He turned to Panya. "Take ten men and return to the shore."

Panya looked at Changa skeptically. "What are you planning, Changa?"

"Despite my hatred of them Belay's sons have influence. We must make sure that we are not interfered with."

"So what are we doing?" she asked.

"We're seizing the docks," Changa replied. "Leave the men on the shore. Let no workers through. You will return to the Kazuri and take command. Fire on any ship or boat that tries to enter the harbor or approach the docks."

Changa stalked away to his horse.

"Where are you going?" Panya shouted.

"To end this once and for all," Changa replied.

He galloped away before Panya could protest, speeding through the narrow Mombasa streets. He crossed the bridge between Stone Town and Country Town but did not stop there. Soon he was riding across open land to a place he'd only visited a few times before. Each visit was an unpleasant event, usually spurred by an equally unpleasant incident. Time after time Changa advised Belay to rein in Naragisi, but the usually stern merchant had a weakness for his sons that defied common sense. They were his legacy, but a man would never choose such a poor heritage to leave behind. Jengo and Niko were useless; Naragisi was dangerous.

Naragisi's mashamba came into view as Changa crested the low hill before him. The Samburu village that served as protection was barren, apparently abandoned long ago. Naragisi seemed to have fallen on hard times but he still managed to raise enough wealth to hire the Samburu to attack Yusef's home.

Changa dismounted, patted his knife bag then descended the hill. He was sure there would be someone waiting for him, for Naragisi was no fool. He knew if his attack failed Changa would come for him. He would be prepared.

Changa took out his sword then crossed the deserted pasture spanning between the abandoned village and the mashamba, careful not to step in scattered piles of dung. Nervousness picked at the back of his neck as he neared the massive home. The Samburu were gone as were the cattle. Whatever Naragisi planned had even driven them away, or killed them. Usenge came to his mind and he sheathed his sword. It would be useless against his minions. Changa extracted two throwing knives from his bag, holding them both in his left hand. There was no reason Naragisi should know of the tebos, but as he learned in the Middle Kingdom distance or ignorance were no hindrance for the foul beasts

"My brother, you've finally come!"

Naragisi's voice echoed around Changa. Changa tightened his grip on his knives as he searched for the foul man.

"As much as I wished your demise you still live," Naragisi said. "You are a hard mtwana to kill. Maybe that is why my father loved you. You've proven to be resilient and quite clever, I must admit. But we all must prostrate before Allah one day. Today is our day."

Naragisi's choice of words did not slip by Changa.

"I see you don't expect to survive this day," Changa shouted back. "You won't be disappointed."

Naragisi's laugh chaffed Changa's anger like rough stone.

"I am already dead, mtwana. You cannot harm me. But my condition is temporary. Once I have your life, all will be well. I will see you soon, brother!"

A deep grunt behind him was his only warning. Changa spun just in time to see the bull charging him. The bovine bellowed as it rammed its head into Changa's midsection. Changa's knives flew from his hands as he tumbled through the air then crashed through the doors of Naragisi's home. The force kept him sliding down the wooden floor until he skidded to a halt against the legs of a waiting Samburu. Changa reacted instinctively, snatching his shimsar free then slashing upward. The blade did not reach its mark, but it did block the spear aimed for his heart. He kicked out, his feet striking the man's shins and sending him tumbling back. Changa jumped to his feet, facing the Samburu with shimsar in hand. Instead of attacking, the warrior's eyes went wide. He leaped into a room to his right.

Changa heard the hooves clattering against wood. He turned in time to see the bull charging him again, its thick wide horns spreading across the hallway. The expression on its face was one of human malice.

"Naragisi!"

He jumped into the room with the Samburu. Their fight was brutal but short, Changa decapitating the man with an angry slash.

"Come out and face me, Changa!" Naragisi roared. "One bull against another, Mbogo!"

His laughter reverberated against the walls. The hallway was too narrow and the rooms most likely hiding Samburu waiting in ambush. Changa could not fight the creature Naragisi had become in the house. He would have to lure him outside. The only way to do so was to enter the hallway and hope he was fast enough.

Changa leaped into the passageway then ran. Throwing spears zipped by him as he passed the rooms, Naragisi's hooves drumming on the floor. His deformed brother was almost at his back as he exited the home; he jumped to his left, but not soon enough. Pain seared across his back as the tip of Naragisi's horn tore his skin. He stumbled to his knees, reaching back to touch the wound. It was bloody but not deep. It would not kill him.

"Changa!"

The voice shouting his name was not Naragisi's. Changa

looked to the house and saw Panya crouching beside the entrance, whip in one hand, sword in the other. He gave her an admonishing scowl that quickly transformed into a sly grin. A Samburu ran through the entrance; Panya's whip wrapped around his ankles. She jerked hard, yanking the man off his feet before decapitating him. Changa turned his attention back to Naragisi. No man would exit the house alive.

Changa and Naragisi circled each other, their eyes locked in wariness and hate. Naragisi feinted and Changa shifted his feet, preparing to evade the attack. A grotesque smile came to the bull man's face.

"You are afraid, mtwana. You should be."

"Why would you do this?" Changa said. "You transform into a beast just to kill me? You still insult your father, even after his death. It is good you've chosen to become an animal. Now I can slaughter you without remorse."

Naragisi charged. Changa stood his ground, assessing Naragisi's new form. He was powerful without a doubt, with muscles likely fueled with nyama. Changa had bested bulls before in his days in the pit, but they were animals of high brawn but low wit. He waited until the man beast was almost upon him before dodging, then striking out with his sword. The blade tip left a seam of blood along its side. Changa and Naragisi danced, Changa avoided Naragisi's desperate charges with grace, leaving a cut or slash with each move. Naragisi panted, his thick tongue hanging from his mouth as he bled over his entire body. Changa braced for another attack; instead Naragisi rose up on his hind legs. He ran at Changa man-like, striking out with his forelimbs and swinging his horns like double blades. Changa stepped back from the onslaught, waiting for his moment. It came when fatigue forced Naragisi to pause. Changa attacked, driving his sword under the rib cage and into Naragisi's lungs and heart. Naragisi bellowed then swung his head hard. The massive horns struck Changa's head. Changa blacked out and tumbled to the ground.

When he awoke he was pinned by Naragisi's bulk, his body slick with blood. Changa shifted then grunted as he strained to free himself.

"Changa! You're alive!" Panya shouted.

"Barely," Changa replied.

Together they pushed the bulk that was Naragisi from atop him. Changa laid still, his body aching everywhere. Panya went to work, wiping the blood from his body then poking and prodding him.

"What are you trying to do?" Changa said. "Finish the deed?"

"Be quiet," she said. "You complain like a child."

Changa grinned then let Panya have her way.

"Nothing is broken," Panya finally said.

"Good. Help me up."

Changa stood with Panya's assistance. They looked upon Naragisi's sprawled form as it slowly transformed back to human.

"What do we do about this?" Panya asked.

"Leave it for the scavengers," Changa answered.

Panya helped Changa onto his horse then together they rode for Stone Town. They arrived to chaos. The beaches and docks teemed with angry Swahili merchants shouting and shaking their fists at the Kazuri. The war dhow sat between the docks and the arriving ships in the harbor, her guns loaded and primed. Changa and Panya slipped unnoticed by the angry throng, their destination Belay's warehouse. A smaller crowd mingled there, for few were concerned with another's wealth. At the center of the crowd stood the Mombasa elders, a group of men known for their piety and wisdom. Changa knew them well, for Belay was an elder and spent much time among them. They looked at Changa not with anger, but disapproval. Changa dismounted then winced as he bowed to them.

A thin man wearing a baggy shirt and striped kokoi

hobbled up to Changa. Despite his frail state, Kazi Wagoni was the most powerful man in Mombasa. His merchant acumen was unparalleled and his faith unquestionable. He eyed Changa up and down before speaking.

"You bring shame to the man that honored you," he finally said.

"No more shame than the men who are his true sons," Changa replied.

"Then your quarrel is with them, not us."

"Is that your opinion, or your decision?" Changa asked.

Kazi grinned as he realized Changa's purpose. He was about to speak when Jengo and Niko pushed forward.

"He is not Swahili!" Jengo said. "Whatever has happened to his dhows this day is his own doing. A mtwana can never walk as a Swahili. Allah has seen to it."

"Allah has nothing to do with this," Kazi said. "It would be best that you remain quiet, Jengo. Your ignorant words do not serve you well."

"My father was an elder, Kazi, just like you," Niko said. "Surely we deserve your respect. Send this animal away. He has attempted being something beyond his station and he has failed."

"It is because of my respect for your father that I'm here," Kazi said. He looked at Changa. "I assume Naragisi is dead?"

Changa nodded. Jengo and Niko reacted, Jengo's eyes narrowing as balled his fingers into fists, Niko collapsing in tears where he stood.

"I feel no remorse for his death," Kazi said. "He abandoned the faith for the ways of the infidel. But Jengo and Niko are respected, and in the eyes of our law you are their brother. Are you satisfied with what you seized today?"

"It doesn't come close to what I lost, but it will suit the needs of my men. If the elders promise that no harm will come to us then I am satisfied."

Kazi nodded. "So be it. Now send your dhow away and let us get back to business."

"This is not fair!" Jengo shouted.

Kazi gave Jengo a sidelong glance. "Go home, Jengo and take Niko with you. Be thankful you are still alive."

The elders went away. Jengo pulled Niko from the ground.

"This is not over, Changa," he threatened.

Changa unsheathed his sword. "It can be. Right now."

Changa's men pressed close to the brothers and their body guards. Jengo's head jerked left and right.

"You still live because I honor your father," Changa said.

"If you truly honored him you'd never killed Naragisi," Niko said.

"I would have killed him long ago if Belay had allowed me. The elders have spoken. Go against their word and you're ruined. You know this."

Jengo and Niko glared at Changa a moment longer before stalking away with their men. Changa and his men sheathed their blades. Changa relaxed then winched as he let the pain and disappointment of the day set in.

"Nafasi?" he said.

The young captain came quickly to his side.

"Wave off the Kazuri. Have them pull into the dock. Send a message to Yusef to let him know we are safe."

Changa trudged into the warehouse, seeking a few moments of quiet and rest. In a matter of hours his future had been shattered. It would take time to put it back together. How, he had no idea.

4

THE NEW SAFARI

Changa felt the nudge but ignored it. He couldn't remember being so tired since his days in the pit. The fatigue was partially physical. So many days had passed since he first set sail from Sofala, so many struggles, so many wonders. Now his dreams lay at the bottom of Mombasa harbor.

"Changa, wake up," Panya urged. "Yusef is here."

Changa rolled onto his side. "So what?"

"He insists on speaking to you."

Changa sat up on his thin cot then ran his hands across his head.

"Unless he has a dhow on his back I don't see the urgency."

"You should speak to him, Changa. He's very upset."

Changa looked into Panya's eyes.

"He's your friend. You should see him," she urged.

Changa waved his hand.

Panya went to the door.

"Come in, Yusef."

The hulking Mikijeni rushed into the room then smothered Changa with a hug.

"Kibwana! This is a most terrible thing!"

Changa fought free of Yusef's embrace.

"It is what it is. There is nothing I can do but move forward."

"Did you kill Belay's sons?"

"I killed Naragisi. The others live."

Yusef stood, his huge body quivering.

"I will kill them!"

Changa stood by his old friend then patted his shoulder. "Leave them be. The elders have sanctioned my taking of their warehouse and pardoned me of Naragisi's death. Jengo and Niko are useless without Naragisi. Don't be surprised if they come to you seeking employment."

"Then I will kill them," Yusef said.

Changa laughed. Yusef's emotions eased his stress but did not solve his problem.

"So what will you do now?" Yusef inquired.

Changa hung his head. "I don't know."

"You could sail to the east again."

Changa shook his head. "I need dhows."

"You can buy them."

"With what? Everything I took from Belay's sons will be distributed among my men. We've sent divers to retrieve items from the Sendibada and Hazina but the harbor is too deep. I will have to trade my way back and that will take time, too much time."

Panya's eyes brightened. "Then you must go to where what you have will be most valuable. You must go to the west."

Changa lifted his head. Now that was an interesting idea. He'd known of the western lands for some time but never considered journeying so far.

"You could go to Bornu!" Yusef exclaimed.

Changa shook his head. "The main trade route to Bornu begins in Mogadishu. I'm not exactly welcomed there."

"There is always more than one way to any destination," Yusef said. The grin on his face told Changa he had more to reveal.

"What do you know, my friend?'"

"Trade flows both ways, as you know," Yusef said. "My journeys take me deep into the interior as the tembos flee my amazing hunting skills."

Changa smirked and Panya rolled her eyes.

"I have come across people who trade with Bornu. They wear clothes and jewels from the west."

"Have you been there?" Changa asked.

"No," Yusef admitted. "I have not, but I'm sure we can find a guide to show us the way."

Changa's interest increased. He didn't have the dhows or the trade for another safari to the east. There was the promise by the emperor of the Middle Kingdom, but he could not plan his future on promises. He needed hard trade and Yusef was offering just that.

"How long do you estimate this safari would take?" Changa asked.

"We'll travel during the dry season. We must cross the Great Lake land before the rains begin and the land floods. We can wait out the rainy season on the high ground then proceed afterwards."

"So this is a year's journey?" Panya asked.

Yusef nodded.

"What do you know of this land?" Changa asked Panya.

"I have traveled far, but not in this land. I followed the trade routes."

There really was no choice. The merchants to the north would not deal with him and Sofala was not promising without his cargo from the Middle Kingdom.

"Then we go to the west," Changa decided.

"Outstanding!" Yusef shouted. "It will be wonderful to be on the road with you again, Kibwana!"

Changa smiled but did not share Yusef's enthusiasm. He was starting all over again.

It took two weeks to gather supplies and porters for the interior journey. Changa dispersed Belay's sons goods to his men who chose to stay in Mombasa or return to Sofala. There was more than enough to satisfy those who decided to stay, but the majority of the crew chose to follow Changa into the west. Those who stayed were too old, too injured or too married to follow. Regret ruled their faces, but Changa was not angry with them. He'd taken too much of their lives; he would ask no more. The baharia gathered items they thought would be most valuable; shells, pearls and the few porcelain plates Changa managed to salvage. There were also spices from the east; Changa paid too much for them but Yusef said they could get much more in the interior. They concentrated on goods that could withstand the journey. Yusef contributed a large share of ivory from his warehouses as well. Changa protested but Yusef would not take no for an answer.

Once the goods were selected Yusef hired porters he knew well for the journey. Changa, Panya and the others set up temporary residence on the outskirts of Country Town, preparing for the new adventure.

Changa hefted the new throwing knife in his hand. It was a good weight and well balanced. The blacksmith Yusef suggested knew his craft well. The quality was close to those he carried with him from Kongo.

He threw the knife at a narrow banana tree. It flew true, digging its blades into the soft bark. He was about to throw a second knife when Nafasi appeared.

"What is it, Nafasi?" he asked.

"Nothing Changa. I just wanted to watch you throw your knives. It is a skill I have always admired."

Changa pulled his arm back and let another knife fly. It struck beside the first knife.

"My father taught me to throw," Changa said. "His father taught him. Every boy in Kongo throws the knives. We hunt small game as boys. Later we learn how to hunt men."

He tossed a knife to Nafasi. The young navigator's eyes widened and he jumped away, letting the knife fall to the ground. Changa laughed.

"It's not on fire," he said.

"I didn't know how to catch it," Nafasi replied. "It has three blades."

"I forgot about that." Changa waved him closer. "The three blades increase the chance of striking your target, but it takes some time to master. Each knife has its own weight and requires its own finesse."

He handed a knife to Nafasi. "Try it."

Nafasi grasped the leather wrapped handle, drew his arm back then threw the iron weapon. It struck the tree handle first then bounced away. Nafasi growled and Changa laughed.

"That was terrible!" Nafasi lamented.

"Actually that was quite good," Changa replied. "It took me three weeks to actually hit the tree when I was a boy and it was a bigger tree."

Nafasi rushed to the tree then retrieved the knife.

"I will try again," he said.

He did more than try again. He tried the rest of the day. Changa stayed with him, giving advice with each throw. He knew now why Mikaili chose Nafasi to train as navigator. He was a determined man willing to work as long as it took to become proficient. A crowd slowly gathered around them. The crew had nothing else to do as it waited to depart for Bornu so it decided to use Nafasi's knife throwing as entertainment. Baharia drummed and droned as Nafasi drew back his throwing arm, then sighed when the knife bounced off the tree. Nafasi seemed oblivious to them. He retrieved the knives then threw them again.

Night drew near when Changa held up his hand.

"That's enough for today," he said. "We can try again tomorrow."

"One more time," Nafasi said.

Changa grinned then stepped away. Nafasi drew his arm back then heaved the knife with a grunt. It spun through the air, hit the tree, and stuck. A loud cheer went up among the baharia;

Nafasi raised his hands in triumph. He trotted to the tree then pulled the knife free.

"Very good," Changa said.

"Thank you, Changa. I know I have a long way to go before I can come near your expertise but I am determined."

"Yes you are," Changa replied. "That arm will be sore tomorrow. See Panya."

"I will." Nafasi trotted over to his friends who greeted him with hugs and teases.

5

THE NDOTO MITI

The sun spread its light over the wide horizon, illuminating the blue sky while wisps of ivory clouds drifted by like dhows on a languid sea. Changa and Panya awoke tangled in each other's arms after a night of lovemaking. Changa grinned as she stroked his head and he ran his hand across her backside.

"We begin again," she whispered.

"Yes we do. I like this beginning better."

"So do I." She kissed his ear.

Changa kissed her full on the lips then gently pushed her away.

"I could stay here forever," he said. "But the safari awaits us."

Panya nodded as she rolled onto her back then stretched like a simba. Changa grinned then dressed. Panya reluctantly did the same, donning her Yoruba garments for the journey. No sooner had they emerged from their house did they see Nafasi waving them over to his fire.

"Good morning," he beamed. "The men are anxious to leave. You think they would be weary after being gone so long."

"They are baharia," Changa replied. "Though I am surprised they're looking forward to walking and riding."

Changa scanned the camp, his eyes falling on Yusef and his family. The big man's children danced about him like performers while Kenja busied herself with the morning meal.

"Get off of your baba," she said. "He is not a tree!"

"It's you that should be climbing on me," Yusef replied.

Kenja huffed while she hid a grin. "Every time I do I get another one those."

Changa chuckled. He gazed at Panya and she gave him a sly wink.

They set off north after a slow morning. Yusef, Panya and Changa led the way followed by Nafasi and the baharia. The porters followed them laden with the bounty Changa hoped would resuscitate his hopes of returning home. For three days they traveled across familiar ground. On the fourth day they entered savanna that while unknown to Changa and his crew was well known to Yusef. The tembo hunter wanted to organize a hunt but Changa disagreed. Time was important and they had more than enough ivory to trade.

After two weeks the trail ended. The caravan set up camp and Changa, Panya and Yusef continued on to explore the next leg on their journey. The savanna ended abruptly, rising rapidly into a series of undulating, forest covered hills. A persistent mist drifted between the trees, giving the hills an impenetrable look.

Changa rubbed his chin, battling with emotions that vacillated between excitement and despair. Yusef's face was more certain.

"I am sorry, Kibwana!" he shouted. "It seems I was a fool to listen to those damned traders. There is no trail here!"

Changa continued to study the hills. "We are here. We should go closer to be sure."

"No," Panya said. "There is something more at work here. There are trails if you look with the right eye."

Yusef face went from despair to confusion. "I have only two eyes. What other eye can there be?"

"A talented eye," Panya replied. "Changa, can you sense it?"

Changa looked at Panya skeptically.

"Use your senses, Changa. You'll see what I see."

Changa looked into the hills again. There was something

unnatural about the mist and how it moved between the trees.

"The trails are hidden by the mists," he finally said. "Someone doesn't want us to pass."

Panya nodded.

"Then maybe we shouldn't," Yusef replied.

"We've come too far to stop now," Changa said.

"No we haven't," Yusef replied. "A dead man can't spend his gold."

"We must take a closer look," Changa decided. "Stay here if you wish, my friend."

Changa and Panya proceeded to the base of the hills. The mist flowed from the forest into the grasses, gathering around their legs. Changa's calves tingled as the mist enveloped them. He looked at Panya, a questioning look on his face.

"I will speak with Oya," she said.

She closed her eyes then whispered. A breeze stirred, pushing the mist back into the forest. The breeze continued until they reached the woods' edge.

"Yusef is right," Changa concluded. We should not enter."

They were turning to leave when the forest roared.

"Run!" Panya shouted.

Changa and Panya sprinted across the grass as a gale burst from the forest, the trees bending like weak grass. Changa felt the mist at his back. He ran faster but the gale moved too swiftly. It engulfed him, his entire body tingling as the mist swirled around him and blinded him. His body stiffened with each step until he was still like a statue, unable to move. Something warm touched his cheek then his body went limp. Hands grasped him then lifted him.

"He is still conscious," he heard a female voice say in accented Swahili.

"It doesn't matter,' a male voice replied. "He cannot move."

"Did you get the woman?" the female asked.

"Yes," the male replied. "She is on my simba."

"Good. We will take them to Zaafarani. She will be pleased."

"What about the giant?"

"He is beyond the mist."

"He may come back with others," the male voice said.

"We will be ready."

Changa drifted in and out of consciousness as they traveled. His eyesight blurry, he could only distinguish bright and dark. For a time they traveled in darkness, then brilliance overwhelmed him. After another cycle of bright and dark his journey came to a sudden halt.

"What is this?" This was a new voice, authoritative in tone.

"We found them attempting to breach the forest."

"You should have killed them," the commanding voice answered.

"Not these two. The woman possesses nyama. She summoned a wind that pushed back our mist."

"What of the man?"

"Touch him."

Changa felt rough hands grasp his wrists. He tried to grab them but he was too weak.

"Amazing. He fights the mist. Zaafarani will be very interested. Take them to her. They will make strong riders."

Changa's journey began again. He drifted for an undetermined time before sensation crept back into his limbs then the rest of his body. He opened his eyes to a blue ceiling painted to resemble open sky. The ground felt cold against his back; he slid his hands across fitted ceramic tiles. Changa sat up then grabbed his head, the dregs of the mist making him dizzy. He finally looked about, discovering a familiar sight. He was in a cell, a well-kept cell but confinement nonetheless. A small torch flickered near the cell door, the smoke escaping through the barred viewport. There was a short bench meant to serve as a bed and what looked like a desk carved into the stone wall beside it. A stool rested by the desk. He looked behind him; there was a toilet as well. This was not a cell for punishment. It was a cell for a prisoner of status.

He stood slowly, and then steadied himself as the dizziness subsided. Changa staggered to the door then peered through the barred viewport. There was another cell opposite his.

"Panya!" he shouted. His voice echoed.

"Changa?" Panya's voice emanated from beside him.

"Are you hurt?" he asked.

"No." Her voice was tense yet strong.

"Good." Changa tried to see down the corridor but couldn't.

"Yusef?" he called out.

There was no answer. Either his big friend escaped the mist or was dead. He hoped for the former.

The sound of rattling metal broke the silence, followed by the clacking of hard soles against stone. Changa stepped away from the portal. A pair of green eyes appeared.

"You should be dead."

The voice belonged to a woman.

"If you say so," Changa replied.

"The mist is poison to humans. Animals can pass through it, but it kills humans. At least most humans."

The eyes continued to stare at him.

"Where are we?" he asked.

"You will find out soon enough." A slit opened at the bottom of the door. A tray slid in, followed by a small gourd of water. The eyes disappeared.

Changa went to the tray. The food was unfamiliar to him, but he knew he needed to eat to conserve his strength. Still, it might be drugged. He went back to the portal.

"Panya, the food?" he asked.

"I don't sense anything I'm familiar with," she answered. "I would think it would not be tainted. If they wanted to kill us they would have done so."

Changa sniffed the tray as if he could detect something foul.

"Killing us seemed to be their original plan."

He pinched what seemed to be meat then put the portion in his mouth. It tasted delicious.

"Whatever it is, it's very tasty."

Changa waited before taking another bite. After no ill effects occurred he continued eating. He finished his meal then downed the water. He slid the plate back under the door then sat on the small cot. There was no use checking the cell for weaknesses; anyone taking the time to protect themselves with poison mist would be very thorough. If he and Panya were to escape this situation, it would take a combination of guile and strength.

The hall rang again with clacking heels. Changa's tray slid away then his door opened. A large, bald man clothed in a leather tunic covered with chain mail entered. He held a hooked short sword and small wooden shield. Though his stance was sure, his eyes showed a hint of fear.

"You come," he said, his Swahili stilted.

The man backed away as Changa strode to the door. As he entered the hallway Changa saw the other guards. A group surrounded Panya's cell, watching her closely as she emerged. The green-eyed woman stood beyond Panya. She was taller than the guards, her athletic frame covered by metal armor shaped to her body. Braided hair fell from under her helmet bordering an attractive but stern face. She paid little attention to Panya; her inquisitive eyes focused on Changa. It was a look he was familiar with, a look he experienced often when he was Mbogo, the pit fighter. This one would bear watching.

"Come," the woman commanded. She turned and strode away. Panya waited until Changa was at her side and they walked together.

"She doesn't like you," Panya said in Arabic. The guards did not seem to understand her words.

"It looks so," Changa replied. "Although I would think since both of us have somehow violated their borders her anger would be more generous."

"It's a good thing," Panya replied.

Changa glanced at her. "Really? You think so?"

"If their attention is on you it gives me time to work on getting us out of this place."

Changa shrugged. "We're still alive, so there is a chance. Let us see what our friend has in store for us."

They followed the woman down the narrow corridor. The other cells were quiet; apparently they were empty. Two more guards flanked the prison door. The woman nodded and they stepped aside, their curious eyes fixed on Changa and Panya as they exited the stone building. They stepped into a scene as strange as it was familiar. Before them loomed a city which reminded Changa of Zimbabwe, but this city was much larger. A stone wall surrounded encased it, its borders obscured by numerous small farms. But it was not the city that captured Changa's attention; it was the sight beyond it. Towering trees ringed the barrier, trees higher than any he'd ever see or imagined. Their trunks spread wider than the thickest baobab; they ascended straight into the sky until their massive canopies bent inward to form a ring over the city that restricted the sun's light.

The woman led them through the city. Despite its size it was surprisingly empty. They passed the occasional walker or merchant, but no large numbers of people fitting a city of such magnitude.

"These people are dying," Panya said.

"Quiet!" the woman said. "If you can't speak Kiswahili, don't speak at all."

They continued to the tallest building in the city. There were more guards, their presence startling to Changa and Panya both. The guards sat on male simbas, the largest simbas Changa had ever seen. The simba looked at them; one let out a low growl. The guards reined the simbas and they stepped aside to reveal a wooden door accented with gold, diamonds, rubies and other precious items. The door swung inward and they entered.

They followed the woman down a dim corridor then into an expansive chamber. In the center of the chamber was a woman on a raised stool. She sat with the grace of nobility, her face held high, her eyes hard. She was a handsome woman, her head graced with a mane of hair that rose over her head like a cloud. A blue silk robe covered her generous body, layers of jeweled necklaces gracing her neck with golden bracelets crowding her wrists. The warrior woman led them to her then bowed.

"So these are the intruders," the woman said. Her voice seemed older than her body, a weary tone holding her words together.

"Yes, malkia," the other answered.

She studied them closer, her eyes lingering on Changa.

"Yes, yes," she mused. "Maybe they are the ones."

"May I speak?" Changa asked.

The malkia jumped back on her stool, startled by Changa's voice.

"It has been a long time since I've heard Kiswahili spoken in such a way," she said. "It is obvious you are from the Outside."

"I am Changa Diop," he said. "This is Panya, my second..."

"And your companion," the malkia finished.

Changa smirked. "You are perceptive."

"No, you are obvious," the malkia said as she smiled back.

"Why have you come here?" she asked.

"Your realm was not our destination," Changa said. "We were seeking a shorter route north to Bornu."

"I know not of this Bornu," the malkia replied.

"It is a kingdom far north of here. We are merchants."

The malkia studied Changa. "You seem more than a

merchant to me, Changa Diop. I would say you are a bit of a warrior as well, maybe even a man of lineage."

Changa nodded. "We are all more than we appear."

The malkia's smile faded. She looked about the room.

"Leave us," she said.

The warrior woman looked puzzled.

"Malkia, is this wise?"

"Leave us!" she shouted.

The woman eyed the malkia suspiciously then signaled to the others in the room. They left single file, glancing at Changa and Panya as they exited.

No sooner did the last person leave the room did a desperate look come to the malkia's face.

"You must save me!" she said.

He sprang from the stool then ran headlong toward them, falling into Panya's waiting arms. Panya hugged her as she sobbed. Changa stared at them both totally confused.

Panya patted her back. "Calm down...child. Tell us everything."

"It's the trees!" she said. "They trapped me here and they will trap you, too!"

"What is she talking about?" Changa asked.

Panya gave him a stern look before turning her attention back to the malkia.

"Where are we?" Panya asked.

The malkia looked into Panya's eyes. Gone was the authoritative countenance. What remained was the pleading stare of childish fear.

"I am not a malkia," the woman confessed. My name is Kendi. We are in my dream."

"That's impossible!" Changa said.

Panya gave him a stern look. "Anything is possible. Nyama is strong here."

Changa folded his arms across his chest. "What are you

talking about?"

"I thought I recognized those trees surrounding this city, now I'm certain. They are ndoto miti," Panya said. "Dream trees."

Changa answered her with a blank stare.

"They are remnants of the First World," Panya said, "the time when gods walked with men. It is said that they were the groves where the gods slept. Any human drawn within them would become part of that god's dream and cease to exist in the real world."

An empty feeling came to Changa's gut. "Are you saying...?"

"No," Panya assured him. "The stories are not always true. But what is true this that we are inside this girl's dreams and only she can free us."

"Girl? This is a woman before us. A mature one at that."

Panya shook her head. "She is a child. We see her as she sees herself in her dream."

"I don't understand these things as you," Changa said. "All I need to know is what we need to do to escape."

"We can't do anything," Panya said. "It's all up to you, Kendi."

"Then we will be here forever!" Kendi said.

Panya stroked her hair. "No we won't. You can leave this forest the same way you came in."

Kendi shook her head. "The trees won't let me. They close together whenever I try. Then Elumba and the simba riders come and bring me back. They pretend to do as I tell them, but they don't. Everyone obeys Elumba."

"The warrior," Changa said.

Kendi nodded.

Panya grasped Kendi's shoulders. "The way out is not through the trees. It's through here."

Panya touched her head. "You must go to sleep. When I awaken you, this world will come to an end and we'll be free."

Changa frowned. "It's that simple?"

"Nothing's that simple," Panya replied. "I will make a potion that will make Kendi sleep. After she is in the dream state, I will awaken her."

"And what will I do?" Changa asked.

"You will stand outside that door and make sure no one comes through."

Changa smirked. "As you said, nothing's that simple."

"Elumba will be back soon," Kendi warned.

Changa nodded. He strode to the door, Panya following. "Lock it behind me," he said.

"I will," Panya replied.

He turned to speak but Panya wrapped her arms around him then kissed him.

"Just in case we fail," she said.

"If we fail then we'll be together forever," Changa answered. "That's not so bad."

He smiled then stepped outside the door. His timing could not have been more perfect. Elumba and the simba riders were returning just as Kendi said. The chamber door slammed shut behind him; Changa heard the locking beams slide into place. He took out his throwing knives then laid him them before him. He extracted his shimsar, waving it from side to side.

"I'll do my part," he whispered. "I hope Panya can do hers."

The corridor shook with the simbas simultaneous roars. They ran at him together, jostling each other in the narrow space. Changa sheathed his sword and snatched up a throwing knife. He hurled it into the chest of the closest simba. The beast stumbled and slowed, causing a collision with its mate. Changa threw another knife which sank into the simba's head, killing it. Before the other simba could untangle itself Changa threw a third knife, striking it in the eye. It howled as it attempted to grasp the knife with its front paws. Changa hefted his last knife, taking careful aim before throwing it. It sank into the simba's forehead. The beast shuddered then fell still.

No sooner had the simba expired did the guards clamber over their still warm bodies. Changa ran to meet them, sword in hand. He twisted away from the spear thrust of the first guard to reach him then spun low as he ducked the sword swing of the other guard close behind. He rose, slicing the second guard across the back then grabbed the spear of the first guard his hand, wrenching it from him. A slice across the guard's neck sent him spinning to the ground; Changa tossed the spear up to change his grip then threw it into the chest of the third guard. More guards came and more guards died, but the number of them slowly pushed Changa back toward the chamber door.

He yanked his sword from the chest of the last guard when Elumba appeared. She strode toward him, sword in one hand and knife in the other.

"Why did you come here?" she said. "You have ruined paradise with your presence."

"Whose paradise?" Changa asked. "There is a girl behind those doors who has been a prisoner far too long, and there is a woman before me who has been alive too long."

Elumba halted, a laugh escaping her mouth that chilled Changa.

"Woman? I am the soul of the trees, Bakonga. I've existed longer than you can imagine. Yes, I know you. I know the one who seeks your death. I care nothing for either of you, yet your death will serve both my purpose and his. So let it be done!"

Elumba leaped the distance between them, her weapons raised to strike. Changa dove below her, trying to reach his knives. His back burned as Elumba's blade cut along his spine. He rolled to the closest simba's carcass then snatched a knife from its head. Elumba was charging again as he took a stance, preparing for her attack. She fell on him like a storm, a blinding force of sword and knife. Changa had not faced such a swift opponent since the

Tuareg. He blocked and parried the best he could but Elumba gave him no chance to attack. He would not kill her, but he didn't have to. All he had to do was delay her until Kendi fell asleep.

Elumba stopped as if she read his mind.

"The girl!" she shouted.

Changa grimaced as Elumba's foot sank into his gut. He fell against a dead simba gasping for air. Elumba ran for the chamber door; Changa managed to regain his breath in time to throw his knife. The blade bit into her calf and she stumbled. He yanked another knife from the simba and threw it. Elumba twisted then batted it aside with her sword. She pulled the other knife from her calf then threw it at Changa, just missing his head. Changa attacked Elumba, who handled him deftly despite her wound. Her eyes danced back and forth between Changa and the chamber door. Changa hoped for a distraction that would help him bring this battle to an end but Elumba was too quick.

"Enough of this!" she shouted. Elumba struck his sword with such force it flew from his hand. She did the same with the throwing knife. She lunged and Changa sidestepped then grabbed her sword hand. The knife flashed for his throat but Changa ducked it. He drove his fist into her gut then grimaced; she was hard like the wood from which she sprang. The blow did have an effect; her grip loosened on her sword and Changa wrenched it from her hand. He locked the knife wielding arm under his then swept Elumba' feet. They crashed to the floor. Changa felt Kintu's Gift rise from his stomach and course through his body, but even with the potion's help his struggle against Elumba was at most even. They grappled, Changa using every move he'd learned in his years in the pit, but Elumba was too strong. She forced her way out of every hold, fighting hard to come to her feet.

Elumba lifted Changa off the ground, her arms gripping him in a painful hug. She ran toward the chamber door. Changa realized what she planned to do; he was to be her battering ram. He twisted to free himself but Elumba's grip was sure. Changa turned his head to see the rapidly approaching door. He jammed his feet to the floor then with a grunt twisted Elumba about. They crashed through the door, but it was Elumba that took the brunt of the blow. They both lay still for a moment, each in some measure of pain. Then Elumba stirred as Changa rose up on his hands and knees. She kicked at him, her heel glancing his chin. Changa grabbed at her feet as she tried to rise, climbed on her back then pushed her back down to the floor. She was about to rise again when she saw the same image Changa spied.

"No!" she shouted.

Panya stood beside the bed, a triumphant smile on her face. Lying close to her side was Kendi. She was fast asleep. Elumba's body stiffened under him; Panya's image blurred into blackness. Changa fell into a dark void, spinning and twisting until suddenly light washed over him. He lay atop a thick branch in a grassy field. Panya sat before him, Kendi asleep beside her. The woman was gone; in her stead laid an eight year old girl. Changa rolled off the wood that had once been Elumba then groaned as he struggled to his feet. The wound along his back burned and his entire body throbbed in pain. He managed to look around him. The city was gone; the only evidence was piles of branches where walls and streets once stood. The towering trees no longer bowed over the scene. They stood straight, the leaves falling from the high branches like rain. Changa became drowsy.

"Changa, no!" Panya shouted. "The trees persist. We must leave now."

She rushed to Changa then shoved a sticky ball in his mouth.

"Chew," she ordered.

He chewed as Panya trotted back to Kendi. The bitter tasting substance pushed back the sleepiness but did not eliminate it. He walked to Panya as she sprinkled a white powder on Kendi's eyes. The girl sat up immediately, blinking her eyes in wonder. He smiled at Panya then jumped into her arms.

"I want to go home!' she cried.

Changa shared a sad look with Panya. There was no telling how long Kendi had been under the thrall of the ndoto miti. Her family was probably long dead.

Changa yawned. "Come, we must go now."

They ran from the grass field and through the sentinel trees. Changa experienced a wave of anger as he passed between the wide trunks, Elumba's face appearing briefly in his mind. He shook the image away, hurrying his steps away from the tainted trees then crossing the tall grasses where the mists once flowed. Yusef stood in the distance, his arms folded across his chest as he tapped his foot. He seemed aggravated as they approached.

"Well? Can we pass or not?" he asked. It took him a moment to recognized Changa's condition and the girl.

"Kibwana? What happened! And who is that girl?"

"Yusef, how long have we been gone?" Panya asked.

"Only a moment," he answered. "You went between the trees then you came out."

Changa and Panya glanced at each other.

"Come,' Changa said. "We will not go this way. We will go around."

"As you wish," Yusef answered. He stretched out his arms then yawned.

"It has been a long day."

Changa's rushed his friend away. The last thing he wished was to be trapped in Yusef's dreams.

6

THE LAKE

Changa closed his eyes then smiled as Panya worked the healing ointment into the cut down his back. The wound caused by Elumba's blade persisted longer than normal, a common occurrence for injuries inflicted by otherworldly weapons. The expedition lingered in their camp longer than planned, allowing Changa time to heal and giving Yusef a chance to conduct tembo hunts to increase his ivory inventory. They camped far away from the tainted grove, but despite the distance Changa's nights were disturbed by strange dreams. The trees reached out to them all.

"We should burn them," Changa said again.

"No," Panya argued. "You have enough enemies among the spirits, Changa Diop. You don't need anymore."

"Think of the people who have perished in those trees," Changa replied. "Innocent folk unaware of what befell them."

"Do not blame the spirits, blame the men," Panya said. "The spirits have always existed. It is we who forget. The ndoto miti have existed since the world was made. It is not our place to destroy what the spirits created."

"Aunt?"

Kendi's timid voice interrupted their conversation. The girl had become Panya's little shadow, following her wherever she went. It was only natural; Panya saved her life. As a woman she had been tall, handsome and regal; as a girl she was stocky, beautiful and unsure. Though her body returned to its former form her eyes retained the knowing gaze of one much older. Her stare made the baharia nervous, some of them whispering that the girl might be possessed with Elumba's spirit. Changa would tolerate none of it. Only he, Panya, Yusef and Nafasi were undisturbed by her.

Panya swept her up into her arms then kissed her nose. Kendi giggled.

"Did you sleep well last night?"

Kendi nodded. "I was in the trees again but I was not afraid. You and uncle were with me."

Changa smiled. He was uncle to her, as was Yusef. Nafasi was brother. Kendi had quickly formed a family around her, never once asking about her true home or parents. She knew that such a life was long ago for her. She would never see it again.

"Ho, ho!" a deep voice bellowed from the distance.

Yusef's hunting party returned. The porters carried four tusks on their shoulders with bags of tembo meat as well. The baharia were prepared; they set up smoking stations earlier that day, anticipating a successful hunt.

Yusef walked up to Changa and Panya with a frown on his face.

"I see time has not changed much, Kibwana," he said with a false grimace.

"I do all the hard work and you lounge about with a beautiful woman rubbing your back and who knows what else."

Changa stood then placed his hands on his waist, scowling back.

"Shall I remind you of all the times I delayed your meeting with Allah, pole pole mtu?"

"And I curse you for it every day," Yusef replied, fighting not to grin.

Kendi stepped between them, her expression revealing her worry.

"Don't fight, uncles!" she pleaded.

Yusef, Panya and Changa laughed. Changa lifted Kendi onto his shoulders, tickling her on the way up.

"Yusef and I ended our fighting long ago," he said. "We

are brothers. Come, let's look at the tusks."

The detour around the forest added weeks to their journey, straining supplies and patience. The baharia were seafaring folk, used to covering long distances in days with a good wind. Though they had traveled on many overland adventures with Changa, this was without a doubt their longest ever.

But soon they were back on course. They entered the Sahel on a cloudy morning, the grasses spreading in every direction dotted by shrubs and small trees. Wildlife abounded, herds of grazing animals scurrying out of their path. The first village they encountered was a disappointment; its market was miniscule and its people poor. They traded a few items for more provisions then continued on. The next village was more promising. They were able to procure horses for riding and asses for provisions, relieving the porters of their duties and freeing their hands for weapons. Changa was pleasantly surprised at how few of the items from their journey across the sea were needed to purchase the mounts.

On their third week in the Sahel they came across their first good trading opportunity. The city sprawled over rolling hills, its limits protected by a mud brick wall. An immense lake shimmered on the horizon north of the city. Changa and Panya rode side by side, Changa scrutinizing the city and the nearby lake. Kendi rode with Panya, hugging her waist. Yusef walked beside them shielding his eyes from the rising sun.

"Is this Bornu?" Changa asked his friend.

"I'm not sure," Yusef replied. "I've never been this far."

Changa looked at Panya and she shook her head.

"I don't know anything of this region."

Changa shrugged. "It doesn't matter. Where there is a city there is trade. I'm sure they see us. If they were hostile we would be under attack."

"Unless they are crafty," Yusef replied.

"That's true." Changa turned in his saddle.

"Nafasi!"

The young navigator rode his small horse to Changa. He stuck his tongue out at Kendi and she laughed before hiding her face.

"Yes, Changa?"

"Panya and I will ride to the city. Prepare our goods."

"Changa, I should go with a few of our brothers. These people may not be peaceful," Nafasi warned.

Changa laughed. "You speak to me as if this is my first safari. Panya and I will be fine. Take Kendi with you."

"No!" the girl said.

"Come now," Panya said. "You can't go everywhere with me. Go to Nafasi."

Nafasi guided his mount near Panya then leaned closed, his arms extended. Kendi reluctantly let go of Panya, letting Nafasi take her to his horse.

"Macharia, Diwani!" Nafasi called out. Two baharia trotted up to him. Changa smiled at his choices. Both men were veterans of their safari to the east. They were good fighters.

"Now you are ready," Nafasi said.

The quartet set out for the city. They'd covered half the distance when the gates opened and a group of riders emerged. To Changa's relief they were unarmed. Changa and Panya reined their horses then dismounted.

The group finally reached them. There were ten in total, each draped in richly patterned tobes. The man is the center was the most elaborated dressed, accompanied by a servant holding an umbrella over his head.

"Welcome," he said in Arabic. "I am Abubakar, lawan of Urhobo."

He gestured toward the city. "We welcome you in the name of Allah."

Changa stepped forward. "I am Changa Diop. We are merchants from Mombasa seeking trade."

Abubakar's eyebrows rose. "Mombasa. I have heard of

your city. It is rare for one to come from such a far place to our humble village."

"Rare for us as well," Changa admitted. "As I said, we seek trade."

"Alas, we are too small a market for a large caravan such as yours," Abubakar replied. "The Mai's wealth does not extend to our land. We give more than we receive. Despite that we extend our hospitality to you. There is a site along the banks of the lake that would easily hold your number. The water is good and we will provide you with what meager food we have."

"Is this Kanem or Bornu?" Changa asked.

"It is both," Abubakar answered.

Changa struggled to hide his disappointment. It had been a long journey and he was keen to profit from it as soon as possible. He was also suspicious that Abubakar did not welcome them into the city. He did have armed men, but they were present to protect their goods. Still, a small city such as Urhobo did well to be wary.

"Thank you, Abubakar," Changa finally said. "We will go to the lake."

Abubakar smiled. "Please follow us."

Abubakar led Changa and the others to the banks of the lake. The expansive body of water reminded Changa of the lakes beyond Country Town, though the landscape surrounding it was not as dramatic.

"I hope you find this site sufficient," Abubakar said.

"It will do fine," Changa replied. "Thank you."

Abubakar nodded. "We will return shortly with food."

Abubakar and his men hurried away. Yusef appeared by Changa's side with a scowl on his face.

"I've never been so insulted in my life!" he said. "He calls himself a good Muslim?"

"I don't know what he calls himself," Changa replied. "I call him cautious. A group of armed men appear from a direction from which no one usually comes. They claim to be merchants yet they have a large amount of armed guards. I wouldn't let us into my city either."

Yusef rubbed his chin. "Still, it is an insult."

"I'll let you worry about Muslim courtesy," Changa said. "The rest of us have a camp to set up."

The camp was erected with the usual efficiency. The water from the lake was not pristine but adequate; a little preparation and a bit of Panya's potions made it drinkable. The sun sat low on the horizon when Abubakar returned with the food he promised. His courtesy may have been wanting but his generosity was opposite. Changa and the others were treated with a feast of goat, sorghum, yams and dates. After a long time on the trail it was good to have fresh food from the farm. Changa sat in a circle with Abubakar, Panya, Yusef and Kendi. They ate heartily, yet Abubakar did not join them.

"We thank you for the food," Changa said.

"It does not make up for the fact that you did not invite us into your city," Yusef commented with his mouth full.

"I understand your feelings," Abubakar answered. "But you must understand mine. It is our way to be cautious. The mai's protection is weak here. We have often found ourselves behind our walls fighting off bandits many times."

"We understand," Changa replied as he cut a mean eye at Yusef. "We will speak of it no more."

Abubakar nodded. "Mombasa is a Swahili city, is it not?"

Changa nodded. "Yes it is."

"It is said the Swahili are good Muslims and great seafarers."

"We are," Nafasi answered proudly.

"There are many treasures to the east, I am told. So why do you come here?"

Changa frowned. "We have been to the east. When we returned we brought much wealth. But fate conspired against us.

I believe the ancestors felt our traveling was not done."

Abubakar nodded thoughtfully. "Well, we are graced with your visit. We hope you rest well tonight before continuing your journey."

Changa smirked. It was a polite way to tell them to be on their way. He agreed; there was no wealth to be made in Urhobo.

The sun had set when the Urhobobu returned to their city, lighting their way with torches. Changa and the others slept quickly, exhausted from the stress of the day. No sooner had his eyes closed did Changa find himself in the midst of a dream that seemed more like a vivid memory…

He beheld a large inland sea. Massive stone buildings rimmed the depths, a band of brick which extended away from the sea into verdant grasslands. Though the surrounding grasses teemed with wildlife, the majestic people inhabiting the sea city turned their backs on the bounty. Their faces and their lives focused on the waters. Thousands of docks extended into the lake, filled with ships and boats of various sizes. The sea was the cradle of all life surrounding it, seething with fish, crustaceans and all forms of water life. In center of the vast sea a ring of marble floated, the perfect circle intersected at precise intervals by towers upon which a perpetual fire blazed. Time sped by Changa's eyes like a gazelle, the transition between dry and rainy season only moments. But then it slowed. Large canoes appeared on the sea, approaching the circle from every direction. Each boat was manned by a team of rowers who kept time with a drum that echoed across the watery expanse. At the bow of each boat a man or woman stood draped in a woven cloak of cotton, their shaved heads crowned in a circle of gold. The boats glided across the calm water to the stone circle. The richly dressed folk climbed from the boats then positioned themselves below the burning torches. The water in the center of the circle stirred; the boatmen began chanting to the rhythm of the drums, their voices rising with the swirling waves. A plume of water shot into the air and hundreds of massive tentacles burst forth. The pale white appendages writhed across the water then grabbed the waiting sacrifices. Just as quick it pulled them below the surface. The water calmed; the boatmen rowed away. Changa's view diminished as the sea cities crumbled, the waters receding until it resembled the lake by which he slept…

"Changa!"

Panya's scream woke him. He slid across the grass toward the lake as did his companions. He looked down to his legs; a wet white tentacle gripped his ankle. Changa grabbed the throwing knife dangling from his belt then hacked at the horrible appendage, determined to cut free. Black fluid oozed from where he struck but the tentacle would not loosen its grip. Panic gripped him as he neared the water, the image of the hapless sacrifices in his head. He began hacking again, cutting his leg as much as he cut the tentacle.

Someone ran by him. Changa looked up to see Kendi. She was free, yet she ran toward the water.

"Kendi no!" he shouted. "Get back! Go the city!"

Kendi looked at Changa. The girl was transforming back into the woman, her body growing with every second.

"They are the ones who did this to us," she said, her voice old like her eyes. She waded into the water.

Changa ceased hacking the appendage.

"Come back, Kendi!" he yelled.

Kendi turned to him then smiled.

"You saved my life, Changa Diop," she said. "Now I will save yours."

Kendi dove into the waters. She swam for a distance then disappeared under the churning surface. Changa continued to struggle with the tentacle as his legs reached the lake edge. He looked at his crew in alarm, everyone battling against the relentless pull of the invisible sea beast. Then the tentacle jerked and the grasp around his ankle loosened. Changa reached down then gripped the unctuous limb with both hands. It pulled away easily. He clambered to his feet, running first to Panya. She struggled in water to her neck, straining to keep her head above water. Changa groped about her until he found the tentacle pulling her down then ripped it away. Others were freeing themselves as he and Panya went about to help.

"Where is Kendi?" Panya asked.

Changa pointed to the lake. Terror gripped Panya's face.

"No," Changa said. "It's not what you think. She's not who we thought."

Sea water churned in the center of the lake. Changa gripped his throwing knife as the water transformed into a black soup. A shock wave rippled across the lake as a large mass burst onto the surface, a grotesque mound of putrid flesh and flailing tentacles. A light glowed beneath it, growing brighter and hotter with each moment. The water boiled about the beast before the light emerged, bringing a semblance of sunrise to the morbid night. The creature scorched under the light's brilliance, the smell of burning flesh forcing them to cover their noses. The beast's carcass broke into flames as did the black ichor around it, a funeral pyre for a creature that had existed far too long. A bright orb of iridescent light emerged from the fire

"Thank you for freeing me,' Kendi said in Changa's head. He looked to Panya, who nodded to acknowledge she heard the voice as well.

"My debt to you is paid. Now I must go. There are others I must deal with. Peace unto you, Changa and Panya. The ancestors are watching."

The orb lingered for a moment then ascended into the sky until fading into the dark and stars.

*   *   *

Changa's camp reeled in confusion. Changa waded through the edges of the lake, making sure everyone was accounted for. His search ended in disappointment and sadness; Iridize and Diwani were missing and three of Yusef's porters were seriously injured.

"Panya!" he called out.

The Yoruba healer limped to his side. She carried her bag of healing herbs, her face distraught.

"Have you seen Idirisi or Diwani?" Changa asked.

Panya shook her head. "They are dead, Changa."

Changa clinched his teeth then sighed. He sat on the lake shore them massaged his forehead.

"Are you tending the injured?" he asked.

"Yes," Panya said as she nodded. "Nafasi and Yusef are gathering everyone."

"Good. Are you okay?"

"I'm well enough," Panya replied. She sat beside him then examined him. Changa's leg was injured, but he was in better shape than her.

"Leave me be," he barked. He swept her up into her arms then carried her to the camp. Yusef greeted him with anger.

"What did those infidels released on us?" he bellowed.

"They claim to be devout then try to feed us to a monster!"

Changa placed Panya down on an empty cot. She tried to rise but Changa shook a finger at her.

"Rest, sweet flower. We will tend ourselves the best we can."

He turned his attention to Yusef.

"We will deal with our host soon," Changa said. "For now we must make sure everyone is safe."

"We will kill them!" Yusef shouted. "Barake, Zufan and Waiyaki were drowned by that thing. They were good men, Changa. What will I tell their families?"

"We may have to deal with them sooner, Changa," Nafasi said.

Changa looked to his navigator, who then pointed toward Urhobo. A faint glow emanated from the city, a sign of lit torches. The gate creaked open and a river of torches flowed rapidly toward the lake.

"Baharia!" Changa shouted. "If you can stand grab your swords! This night is not done!"

The baharia scrambled to their weapons, grabbing their swords and knives then slipping quickly into their chain mail. They followed Changa as he strode toward the approaching wave, shimsar in one hand, throwing knife in the other. He was flanked by Yusef and Nafasi.

As he neared the Urhobobu his stride slowed. These were not warriors coming to them; these were ordinary men and women, young and old, staggering to them with expressions of relief and joy. Changa raised his hand.

"Lower your weapons," he ordered.

The people swarmed them with praise and gratitude, dropping to their knees then sprinkling their heads with sand.

"What are they doing?" Changa asked.

"They are showing us honor," Yusef replied. "It is their way in the west."

Changa knelt before an old woman hiding her face in the sand, her mumbled praises barely audible.

"Please aunt, do not do this," he said. "We deserve no praise."

"But you freed us," she said. "You freed us!"

She wrapped her feeble arms about his neck then kissed his cheek.

Abubakar and his entourage arrived moments later. Guilt was clear on the leader's face. Before Changa could react Yusef rushed up then punched Abubakar, knocking the lawan on his back.

"You would feed us to a monster?" he yelled. He took out his scimitar then raised it to strike. Abubakar's men did nothing, looking at Yusef with resignation.

"Yusef, no!" Changa called out.

Yusef looked at him incredulous.

"He tried to sacrifice us! My friends are dead because of him!"

"My brothers are dead, too," Changa replied. "There will be no more killing this night."

Yusef glared at Changa. Changa's eyes narrowed.

"Put down your sword, Yusef. Now."

Yusef lowered his sword. He spat on the ground near Abubakar then stalked away. Abubakar stood, dusting off his tobe.

"He has reason to be angry. We deceived you."

Changa did not answer. It took all his effort from running his sword through the man.

"The lake jinn has terrorized our city for generations," Abubakar explained. "Its power was just not physical, it was mental as well. Did you have the dream?"

"Yes," Changa replied.

Abubakar closed his eyes. "Be thankful it was only one night. For our people it is a curse we cannot escape. But you have freed us of it, and for this we are grateful."

Changa said nothing. The loss of his brothers weighed heavy on him.

"There is nothing we can do to ease your loss," Abubakar continued. "Please accept this gift in hopes that it will benefit you on your journey."

Abubakar turned to his men, gesturing them forward. The men came forward, caring a weathered ebony wood box between them. Another man followed them, his young face resembling Abubakar's. He was richly dressed; a jeweled sword hung from his waist.

"This is our most precious possession. It is valued more by the Mai than it is by our own. Take this to him and he will be generous. My son, Jafaru, will accompany you to insure you are welcomed."

Changa grinned. Jafaru was to be their royal hostage. The man seemed unfazed by his status, though Changa knew that might change once they neared the capital city.

"Nafasi!" The young navigator came to his side. The look he shared with Abubakar was not pleasant.

"Abubakar offers us a gift," Changa said. "Take it and place it with the other merchandise. Jafaru will accompany you."

The baharia took the box. Nafasi and Jafaru followed them into the darkness.

"You must understand my decision," Abubakar said. "A lawan must protect his people."

"I don't wish to speak any more of this," Changa said. "We accept your gift. Now leave us. All of you."

Abubakar and his guards rounded up the villagers then led them back into the city. Changa turned his attention back to his people. Panya was on her feet again against Changa's advice, assisting the injured despite her own injuries. Nafasi and the others assisted as they could. Everyone avoided Jafaru. The only person interested in him was Yusef, and his eyes betrayed his intent.

Changa walked over to the Urhobobu prince.

"Come with me," he said. "You'll help with the wounded."

"I must protect the talisman," he replied. "It is my duty."

"You'll come with me, or that man over there will kill you," Changa said. He pointed at Yusef. Jafaru's eyes widened.

"I will go with you," Jafaru answered.

Changa, Jafaru and the others toiled throughout the night then slept through the early morning. By afternoon they were on their way, eager to be away from the lake and the city. Jafaru rode close to Changa and Panya; Yusef chose to stay close to his companions. There was a strained silence between the three until Changa's curiosity got the best of him.

"Where are we headed?" he asked.

"Birni Ngazaragamo," Jafaru answered. "It means the walled fortress in our language. It is the capital city of Bornu."

"What makes this talisman so special?" he asked Jafaru.

The young prince eyes brightened. "Kanuri rule over our region is new, Kanem was a great empire, but nobles constantly fought each other for control. Mai Dunama, desperate to gain advantage over his rivals, opened the talisman hoping the ancestors would aid him. They did not. Instead the empire crumbled as the ancestors turned against him. The Bulala, the people of the lake, drove the Kanuri south. The talisman was lost, or so everyone thought."

"How did your people end up with it?" Changa asked.

"Our family took the talisman from the Mai during the civil wars following the Bulala victory. We vowed to keep it until the Kanuri won the ancestors favor again. It seems as though they have."

"And what's in it for us?" Changa asked.

"Sultan Ali Ghajedeni will be generous," Jafaru said with a smirk. "Very generous."

Changa smiled his first smile in days. Finally this safari was about to pay off.

"This it's on to the walled fortress!" Changa shouted. The baharia shouted in response. Their luck was finally changing for the better.

-END-

KITABU CHA NANE

(BOOK EIGHT)

THE NYAMA BOOK

1

THE CAGED KING

The City of Birni Ngazaragamo sprawled across the Sahelian grass, encased by a stout wall surrounded by sorghum fields, scrub trees and solitary baobabs. The city roads were thick with traffic, farmers leaving their compounds to work their fields and merchant leading camels and donkeys loaded with goods. Changa smiled broadly upon seeing the activity. So far the safari had only yielded enough goods to sustain them. Maybe now they would make the profits they sought.

Panya rode by his side, her solemn mood persisting. Changa reached out, touching her cheek. She turned to him and smiled.

"You worry about me," she said.

"I do," he replied. "It's not your way to be so glum. Serious maybe, but not glum."

"It will pass," she answered. "I think I'm becoming road weary."

Changa nodded. "I understand. We have traveled many miles. I wrested you from a settled life in Mombasa and heaped all this trouble on you. I promise you that this is our last safari."

Panya looked at him skeptically. "You say that now only to comfort me. But it doesn't. If this is your last safari it means you have what you need to fulfill your promise. That does not make me feel better, Changa Diop."

His attention was distracted by a commotion at the nearest gate. A group of horsemen carrying spears and flags galloped toward them.

"Changa!" Jafaru called out. "The mai sends his escort. It is time you played your role."

Changa gave Panya a long look before taking his place beside Jafaru. The men approaching them wore chain mail and white turbans. They held double headed lances in their right hands while guiding their mounts with their left. Leather quivers filled with fletchless arrows bounced off their backs.

"This doesn't look like a welcoming committee to me," Changa commented.

"The mai likes to show his strength," Jafaru replied. "His peers are a restless lot. They often challenge his rule. A warrior of the mai is kept very busy."

The parties halted a few yards from each other. Changa rode forward with Jafaru and his attendants; one of the horsemen broke from the ranks and met them.

"Welcome, Urhobobu," the man said. The tone in his voice was not hospitable.

"I am Jafaru, son of Abubakar, mai of Urhobo," Jafaru said, his voice full with authority. "This is Changa Diop, Swahili chief of Mombasa. We have come seeking council with Mai Ali."

"There are many who seek council with our blessed mai," the man replied. "We will take you to the city and provide you lodging. Whether or not you see the mai is in Allah's hands.

"We are thankful for your consideration," Jafaru said. "Please inform the mai that I wish to share with him that which binds us all."

The warrior's eyes narrowed. He looked past Jafaru to the wooden chest carried by his servants.

"Follow me," he said.

The warriors escorted them through the gates of Birni Ngazaragamo. The innards of the city were similar to Urhobo, mud brick walled compounds mingled with individual cone shaped buildings with grass roofs. Changa's observant eyes assessed the valuables available in the markets they passed and was pleased. This would be a good venture. He saw nothing of the merchandise he carried, no porcelain, ivory, or cowries. He would have a monopoly, which was always good for prices.

The mai's compound occupied the city's center. The expansive compound possessed its own market, a lively gathering of carts, merchants and buyers occupying a wide area to the left of the compound gates. Warriors dressed similar to their escorts flanked the elaborate wooden palace gate while archers patrolled the ramparts, looking down on the market with indifference. The compounds of the mai's council lay to the right of the gate; those of visiting dignitaries lay to the left. Their escorts guided them left.

"Where are we going?" Jafaru said.

"We are taking you to your compound where you will await the mai," the man answered.

"I am the son of Abubakar! You will place me among foreigners?"

"I'm taking you where the Mai wishes you to be," the escort leader said. "There you will remain until the mai determine otherwise. Many have come claiming to have what you say you have. If what you say is true you will be honored. If not, you will be punished. Such is the mai's will."

Jafaru looked at Changa in confusion. Changa glared back at him. Panya and Yusef came to his side immediately.

"What's going on?" Panya asked.

"Our claims are apparently being challenged," Changa replied. "It seems we're on probation until their ruler determines otherwise."

"I knew we shouldn't have trusted him!" Yusef said. "We can still fight our way out."

"No," Changa said. "I think Jafaru is in more danger than we are. For now we will do as they say."

Changa rode forward to Jafaru then addressed the escort captain.

"We thank you for the mai's hospitality. I'm sure that once he examines our claim he will be pleased."

The escort seemed to relax. A weak smile came to his face.

"This one knows his place," the captain said. His eyes shifted to Jafaru. "You could learn from him, Bulala."

Jafaru opened his mouth but Changa touched his shoulder. Jafaru jerked his head toward the Bakonga.

"I know you are insulted," Changa whispered. "But now is not the time for pride. Once the mai confirms your claim you'll get the respect you deserve. For now, go slow. This man is your only contact between you and the mai. Your actions will precede your presence. They will define you."

Jafaru nodded.

"We are thankful for the mai's hospitality," he finally said to the escort captain.

"Where are you taking us?" Jafaru asked.

The captain grinned. "The Songhai compound."

Jafaru's eyes went wide. "The Songhai? What is…?"

Changa touched his shoulder. "Patience," he whispered.

"As you wish," Jafaru replied. His face looked as if he'd swallowed a frog.

The Songhai compound was the last compound in the foreigners' district and the furthest away from the mai's palace. The walls displayed obvious neglect; no guards protected the battered gates. As they entered the inhabitants studied them with curious eyes; Jafaru looked at them with disdain. Changa considered their temporary neighbors with a merchant's eye and was pleased by what he saw. The Songhai stood in sharp contrast to their surrounding, richly dressed people festooned with gold and other jewels. The stable was crowed with camels and asses, a sign of a large caravan loaded with goods.

The escort led them to their abode. It was a large home, the largest in the compound. At least the mai recognized Jafaru's status among the foreigners.

"I will return tomorrow," the escort said. "Allah be with you until then."

He and the others rode away. Changa immediately set about getting his people in order.

"Nafasi, unload our goods then get everyone settled. We'll store the ivory inside."

Nafasi nodded then shouted orders to his brothers. Panya came to his side.

"These Songhai are interesting," she commented.

"Very," Changa replied.

Yusef joined them.

"By the looks of it I would say they are far wealthier than these Kanembu."

"I agree," Changa replied. "But we only see the best of them now."

"They are fish eaters," Jafaru said in a way that made clear his statement was an insult.

"They claim to be good Muslims but they hide their blasphemy under their vain robes. Their mai is a witch."

"Such things don't concern me," Changa replied. "I am here for trade, not faith."

"You should be wise about who you deal with, Swahili."

"And you should be wise about who you insult," Changa said. "Your father is not here to protect you, not that he could put much of a showing based on what I saw. You are of lineage, but that only matters as long as those more powerful than you choose to honor that. To a thief on the road you're just another man to rob."

"It seems we have visitors," Panya commented.

A man approached, draped in a red and yellow robe, his head wrapped in a red turban. He grinned as he bowed to them.

"Welcome to our compound," he said. "I am Sibiri Traore."

Jabaru did not reply. He brushed by the man then went into the compound.

"I am Changa Diop. This is Panya Ajala and Yusef Mataka. We are merchants from Mombasa."

The man nodded in acknowledgement but his eyes lingered on Panya as the eyes of men often did.

"You are Yoruba," he said.

"Yes," Panya replied.

Sibiri rubbed his beard. "Interesting. A Kanuri traveling with Swahili and a Yoruba housed in a Songhai compound. Your friend must have done the mai a great wrong."

Changa was feeling less secure about their situation.

"What do you know of such things?" he asked.

Sibiri smiled. "We Songhai are not especially loved here. Yes, we trade, for business knows no boundaries, but our realms are continuously at odds. The Kanembu push west and we push east. But then I am just a merchant. Please feel at ease, Changa Diop. Maybe once you are settled we can take stock of each other's goods?"

"Yes. Maybe we can," Changa said. Now this was more to his liking.

Changa and the others settled in for a restful sleep. The next morning they cooked breakfast in the center of the compound, Changa, Panya, Yusef and Nafasi sharing a meal together.

"We have stepped into a hornet's nest," Yusef said.

"It seems so," Changa replied. "But we are here now. We must avoid being stung."

"The Songhai says Jafaru is in ill favor," Panya commented. "I wonder if his people committed some transgression to obtain the talisman."

"You know this land better than us," Changa replied.

Panya munched on a yam. "It's been a long time since I passed through. I didn't linger long. The land is full of mais, each the ruler of his own domain. They pay homage to Ali for his clan is considered the most high. He grants goods and gold to his nobles and those close to him. Jafaru's people are out of his reach and if the escort words are true, they are Bulala. The Bulala revolted against the Kanembu long ago. They are considered the reason the Kanembu lost control of their empire and had to move west."

Changa nodded. "If we could leave now we would, but Ali expects us at his court. We won't linger afterwards. Nafasi, prepare to leave as soon as we return. Hopefully it will be a peaceful exit."

The warrior escort appeared at noon. It was a larger group led by the same captain that escorted them into the city. Changa, Panya and Yusef were garbed in their best robes and adorned with jewels they brought from Mombasa. Changa also took the time to gather a sampling of goods from the Middle Kingdom. If things went bad he would bribe their way out of the city. If not, he was prepared for other means.

Jafaru was the last to emerge from the compound. He kept to himself throughout the night, suffering only the company of his attendants. When he stepped out into the Kanem heat Changa groaned. The young prince resembled a mai himself; his layered tobes bloating him to twice his width. The topmost tobe shone royal purple and sparkled with gold thread patterns. A purple turban rose from his head like a baobab, held together by an onyx broach. His attendants were equally resplendent, one carrying the parasol, the other an ornate drum. Changa shook his head as he approached Jafaru.

"You look wonderful," Changa said. Jafaru nodded, his pride evident on his young face.

"However I fear you may look more like a rival than a supporter."

Jafaru frowned. "I am son of a mai, a chiroma. I will not deny my status to satisfy another's sinful vanity, no matter who they are."

It was too late to argue. They followed the escort to Ali's compound. At the gate they were relieved of their horses. The escorts led them single file into the compound then into Ali's palace. The building was simply furnished as was the way of the most devout Muslims, the walls covered with hanging rugs of local and Persian origin. The corridor opened into an expansive room. An enormous rug covered the floor. Ali's personal guard lined the wall on either side of the room wearing chain mail and low metal helmets. Each man held a small round shield and the double headed lances the Kanembu were noted for. Curved sabers hung from their sashes.

The elders' council sat on the carpet, a gathering of men and women dressed as richly as Jafaru. Their faces reflected their skepticism, their eyes heavy with disdain as they stared at Jafaru. Behind them, flanked by his great wife, queen mother, his chiroma and his closest advisors was Mai Ali. He sat in the fadanir, the royal cage, his back turned to everyone. Jafaru knelt, making the gesture of sprinkling sand on his head. Changa and the others repeated the gesture.

The person who finally spoke was not the mai but his gesere. He was a man who despite his layered robes still appeared thin.

"Welcome Jafaru, son of Abubakar," he said. "The mai is grateful for your presence. I hope your journey was safe and your accommodations acceptable."

"I thank the mai for his hospitality," Jafaru replied. Changa was relieved the young man ignored the insult.

"You bring a word from the lake," the thin man said.

Jafaru nodded. "I have come on my father's behalf. The lake jinn is dead, slain by those who accompany me."

A murmur coursed through the elders. Changa saw the mai turn his head slightly upon hearing the news, though not so much to reveal his face to those unworthy of seeing it.

"It was foretold long ago that when the lake jinn died the

curse upon the Kanuri would end," Jafaru continued

"You speak of curses like an infidel," one of the elders commented.

"I speak of our history, something many seem to have forgotten the moment they opened the Koran," Jafaru replied.

Changa closed his eyes. The arrogant Jafaru had returned.

Jafaru stood. "It is said when Dumana opened the sacred talisman to defeat his brethren, he caused the collapse of the Kanembu. The Bulala pushed us to the south and the talisman was though lost. But such was not the case. True, the Bulala triumphed, but the talisman was given to those who would keep it safe. Now those who have guarded it return it in hopes that Mai Ali will be more prudent than his ancestors."

Jafaru waved his servants forward. They carried the box to the elders then set it before them.

Before the thin man could speak a deep resonant voice responded, the voice of Mai Ali.

"Bring the box to me."

Two of the mai's personal bodyguards hurried forward, picked up the box then took it to the fadanir. They stepped away, immediately prostrating on either side of the cage. The hinges creaked and the door swung open. Everyone in the room immediately prostrated except Jafaru, Changa and the others. The mai emerged from his royal cage then opened the box. He sat still for a moment as he inspected the contents of the box. He closed the box and then reentered the fadanir. The door closed and the others rose from their subservient postures.

"It seems the son of Abubakar speaks the truth. This is the talisman," Mai Ali said.

The elders nodded in approval, but their expressions were no less judgmental.

"We are grateful the Uhborobu have returned such an important object to us. We have not forgotten our entire heritage.

We also honor your companions for freeing our subjects from the terror of the lake jinn. Mai Ali intends to show his gratitude to you all. For now, accept our sincere thanks. May Allah be with you."

The gesere gestured toward the corridor, indicating that their meeting with the Mai was over. Changa and the others prostrated then filed out of the chamber. The escorts led them back through the streets then to the Songhai compound.

"Tonight you will feast at the palace," the escort said.

"Will the Mai attend?" Jafaru asked.

The escort looked insulted. "Of course not. He is the mai."

The man spun about then stomped away. He mounted his horse, glared at Jafaru then rode away, his men close behind.

"You seem determined to aggravate your master," Changa commented.

"He is not my master,' Jafaru replied. "He is a mai, no less and no more than my father. Yet he acts as if he's seen heaven."

"Still, it does not bode well to spit on anyone's hospitality, especially the mai's."

Jafaru walked away. Panya and Yusef joined Changa.

"We should have killed him and his father," Yusef said.

"He is an arrogant one," Panya said. "But death is too harsh a punishment. A certain potion would teach him a lesson though. It would make him retch until daylight."

Changa chuckled. "We'll get our pay from the mai then part ways. We're done with Jafaru. What happens to him afterwards is in Fate's hands. I doubt if he makes it back to Uhboro."

The escort returned that afternoon, taking them to the feast. The banquet was held in the marketplace before the palace. It was a formal, emotionless affair done more out of obligation than appreciation. None of the elders or other dignitaries of the city spoke to Changa and the others. The only thing they shared was disapproving looks. Jafaru seemed immune to the sour attention, eating the mai's food with relish. When they returned to the compound he went immediately to his sleeping chamber.

Changa gathered his people around him.

"Sleep with your weapons tonight,' he advised.

"What is wrong?" Nafasi asked. "Do you not trust the Songhai?"

"I don't trust the Kanembu," Changa replied. "Like I said, keep your blades close. We'll leave an hour before daybreak."

"Jafaru won't be pleased," Panya said.

"Damn Jafaru!" Changa snapped. "He's the one who created this foul mood. Because of him we won't get to lighten the Songhai's purses. The sooner we get away from him the better."

Panya came to his bed that night. She'd been distant of late, but dispelled any worries he may have had when she disrobed on her way to him then kissed him fiercely. Afterwards they lay together, Changa gazing at the grass roof as he slid his hand up and down her back.

"I thought I'd done something to anger you," he said.

Panya shifted against him. "Why?"

"You've been distant."

"You could have asked me."

"That's not my way. I assumed you would tell me. That's your way."

"It's not you, it's this place," she said. "Kanem is not far from Yorubaland. My mind is filled with old memories, many of the unpleasant."

"Should we not have come here?" he asked.

"We are where we should be. If not Oya would have told me."

Changa grinned. "So she speaks?"

"I am her daughter, and here we are close to her. You were wise to tell the men to sleep with their weapons. This mai can't be trusted."

"I don't know what it is between Jafaru and these folks,

but it's obvious they don't like each other. There's much malice behind the formality."

He pulled her closer. "It's of no matter. We'll be on our way tomorrow. I hope the mai's gift is generous. Maybe we should go to Yorubaland."

Panya stiffened. "No."

Changa sat up. "You don't wish to go home?"

Panya sat up then dressed. "If I was meant to be in Yorubaland I would be there. Oyo is no longer my home."

"Don't you miss it?" he asked.

"Do you miss Kongo?"

Her words were meant to wound him, and they did. This moment was done. It was then when he smelled burning grass. He jerked his head up and spotted smoke seeping through the woven grass.

"Get out now!" he shouted to Panya. They grabbed their clothes and weapons then fled their house. Outside flaming arrows arched over the compound wall, some landing on the grass roofs, others into the sand. Changa and Panya dressed then ran into the other homes awakening the baharia and the Songhai.

They gathered in the center of the compound.

"Nafasi, secure our goods and make ready to escape," Changa said. "We'll form a vanguard and make for the gate."

"We'll have to fight our way through the city," Yusef said.

"Either that or burn to death here," Changa replied.

"We must do this together," Sibiri said.

"Yes, we must," Changa agreed. "Do you have fighting men among you?"

"Of course. Between the Tuaregs and the Shuwa a caravan would be foolish not to."

"How many are archers?"

"All of them," Sibiri replied. "They are Songhai."

"Good. We'll station them around the compound

entrance. Yusef, Panya and I will act as the vanguard. Once the archers fire a few volleys we'll charge into them. The other must be ready to follow us. Take only that which you can easily carry."

"But that means…" Yusef began to say.

"…we'll have to leave your ivory behind," Changa finished.

Yusef shook his fist to the sky. "I hate Kanem!"

Nafasi rounded up the archers, positioning them on either side of gate. Changa, Panya and Yusef rode up to the gate, halting a few yards away. They were joined by Sibiri and ten Songhai, their sabers drawn.

"Thank you for your help," Changa said.

Sibiri nodded. "You'll have a chance to thank me later."

Changa looked at the Songhai and smirked. "I suspected so."

Nafasi rushed up to the gate, grasping the handle. His eyes met Changa's. Changa nodded then Nafasi swung the gate open.

Kanembu horsemen rushed in, their lances lowered. The Songhai bowmen and the Swahili baharia released their arrows and men and horsemen fell quickly under the furious volley. The bowmen loaded then released another volley before scattering from the momentum of the horsemen. Changa and the riders plunged into the confusion, hacking down the lancers and driving them outside the compound. The Kanembu abandoned their lances for their swords. As the baharia rushed to their horses to escape, the Songhai archers lingered. They manned the ramparts of the compound wall, firing into the Kanembu as the vanguard cleared the compound entrance.

"Push them from the road!" Changa yelled.

Changa and the Songhai wheeled right, driving the Kanembu into the walls. The merchants rushed out, flanked by the archers. They rode hard down the wide streets, the archers driving back anyone that dared approach them.

"They're clear!" Panya shouted. She cracked her whip on the face of a Kanembu attempting to dismount her and the man fell away screaming.

The riders broke off their attack then galloped after their cohorts, the Kanembu close behind. More Kanembu cavalrymen appeared, emerging from alleys and streets beyond the compound. Changa and the others pushed their horses hard, hoping to avoid being cut off from the others. As they neared the main gate they saw archers running on the ramparts hoping to thwart their escape.

Changa veered his mount toward the ramparts.

"Changa! No!" Panya pleaded. "We can make it!"

Changa ignored Panya's cry. He rode to the mud brick stairs leading to the ramparts. His horse hesitated until Changa drove his heels into its flanks. The horse snorted then climbed the stairs. It ran toward the gate, Changa slashing at the archers and driving them either over the wall or off the ramparts into the courtyard. He was proud of himself until he saw the gap between the gate and the ramparts on the other side. He pulled back on the reins but the horse refused to heed. It raced full gallop toward the gap, ignoring every attempt to make it stop. Changa braced himself for the fall; instead the horse leapt the gap, landing nimbly on the other rampart. It continued running and Changa resumed his carnage as if the entire incident was planned. When the horse reached the opposite steps Changa forced it down.

They bolted for the gate. Kanembu warriors rushed at him from all sides, throwing lances, loosing arrows and yelling curses. A group rushed for the gate; if they could not stop the others they would at least catch the one that made good their escape. Changa watched his escape route grow smaller and smaller. The horse, as fast as it was, would not make it.

"Allah give me strength!'

Changa grinned as the gate stopped then began to reopen. Yusef squeezed his bulk through the gap then immediately attacked the warriors at the gate. Changa rode up to him, reining the horse to a halt. Yusef lifted his bulk onto the horse and it snorted in protest.

"Why must your worry me, kibwana?" Yusef said.

The horse hobbled out of the city. Good fortune continued to smile on them for Yusef's horse was nearby. Together they galloped away, eventually catching up with Panya and the Songhai. Panya worked her mount next to his then grabbed his hand.

"You worried about me?" he asked.

"Of course not," she replied. "I worried about Yusef. You cause him so much trouble."

"Indeed he does," Yusef said. "Sometimes I wish you'd have stayed in the East."

Changa glanced behind them. The Kanembu were not giving chase. He slowed his horse as did the others.

"Where are we headed, Sibiri?" he asked.

"To the river," the Songhai replied. "Where else would fish eaters go?"

2

ON THE ISSA BER

The fatigued escapees finally ended their flight at the banks of a wide river. Changa slid off his horse then sat beside it, his body aching from his efforts. The horse sauntered to the river as did the other beasts, indulging in the brown waters. Panya trudged over then sat beside him.

"Our luck seems to waver still," she said.

"No reason to speak the obvious," he replied. "At least we salvaged our most valuable cargo."

"So what do we do now?" Yusef asked. The big man loomed over him, his face upset. "I left a fortune in tusks in that damned city."

"You're welcome to go back," Changa said. "But you'll go alone."

Sibiri came to them. The Songhai merchant smiled as was his way.

"You will come with us to Songhai," he said. "Whatever you have will be of great value there. I think you will find my land much more favorable than Kanem."

Changa stood then dusted the sand from his clothes.

"I'd like a word with you, Sibiri," he said.

The merchant nodded and the two walked to the river's edge.

"What is it you want from us?" he said.

"Can't a merchant help brethren as a friend?"

"We are not friends, at least not yet. As I asked before, what do you want from us?"

Sibiri's smile faded. "I know a person that would be very interested in your services."

"And what services would that be?"

"You slayed a jinn," Sibiri said. "That is something most men can't claim."

"I did not slay it," Changa admitted. "There was one among us who possessed those skills."

"And who is he?" Sibiri asked.

"She...it is no longer with us."

Sibiri looked thoughtful. "So you didn't kill the jinn, yet you traveled with one that had the ability. That still marks you as special in my eyes."

Changa shrugged. "I have confronted many strange things during my safaris. It doesn't make me eager to confront more."

"Let us speak as men, Changa. You've traveled a very long way to trade. I know many ambitious merchants, but none as ambitious as you. I would guess your ambition is fueled by a bit of obligation...and desperation."

Changa didn't answer. Sibiri was a perceptive person, too much so for his taste.

"If what you say is true, what does it have to do with your friend?"

"There is something he wishes of which he would pay most handsomely for."

"So you say," Changa replied.

"So I know."

Sibiri reached into his pouch then extracted a red cloth. He opened the cloth to reveal a jeweled necklace possessing largest diamond Changa had ever seen, bordered with ruby encrusted gold.

"I was instructed to give this to the person I deemed worthy to complete my friend's task. The payment once the task is complete would be ten times this."

Changa opened his hand and Sibiri handed him the bauble.

It rested heavy in his palm.

"What makes your friend believe that I wouldn't keep whatever he wishes me to find if it is so valuable?"

"Its value is not in what it is, but what it contains. Its use is only for a few, of which you are not. To you it would be useless but to my friend it's worth a fortune."

Changa tossed the jewel from hand to hand. "This sounds like a dangerous task. I'm not one to take on anything unless I know who I'm dealing with. You seem to be a good man, Sibiri, but I'm no one's servant. If your employer wishes me to take on this task I must meet with him personally."

Sibiri nodded. "I agree. We shall leave for Songhai today."

Changa held up his hand. "Wait. I must consult my crew."

Sibiri took on a perplexed expression. "What is there to discuss? You tell them what to do and they do it."

"It's not our way," Changa said. "Yes, I am their leader, but I only lead those who wish to follow. I always give them a choice."

"Have they ever refused?" Sibiri asked.

Changa grinned. "No."

"Then they are truly loyal to you. This is a rare thing."

The two men returned to camp. Changa took the baharia aside then explained to them Sibiri's proposal. Yusef was the first to respond.

"I have lost enough on this safari," he said. "It is time I returned home. Maybe I can take more ivory on the way back to make up for what I lost in Kanem."

"Or you can go with us to Songhai," Changa said.

Yusef walked up to Changa and placed his heavy hand on his shoulder.

"Allah knows I love you like a brother, Kibwana. I have brought you this far hoping it would help you regain your wealth. I have failed. This Songhai man dangles a treasure before your eyes with no guarantee you will collect it. I think it's time we all went home."

Panya touched Changa's other shoulder.

"His words make sense, Changa. Maybe it's time we..."

"No," Changa said. "If you wish to return to Mombasa or Sofala that's your choice. I will go on. I have to."

He looked at Panya as he spoke. He knew her opinion had nothing to do with wealth. She did not want to go near Yorubaland.

"I will stay with you," she finally said.

"As will I," Nafasi said. "I speak for myself and the baharia. You have never led us wrong, Changa."

Yusef rubbed his beard as he reconsidered. "I've gone far enough. I have my family to think about."

Changa smile at Yusef. "I know, my friend. I will ask no more of you."

"We shall leave in the morning," Yusef said.

"Take the route through Mogadishu," Changa advised. "The Kanembu will be less hospitable. You can take some porcelain with you. It will trade well there."

Yusef's eyes widened. "You are too generous, Kibwana!"

"I owe you much more, Yusef. We will speak no more of this."

Sibiri approached Changa. "I knew it would be as such. Now we must plan our journey to Songhai."

"Is it a long journey?" Changa said.

"On land, yes. But we will not take the land route. We will use the river."

Sibiri led them to the riverbank. The Songhai servants dug along the bank, the sun glistening on their bare backs. Minutes later the outline of hulls appeared.

"We are always ready for any contingency," Sibiri said. "We are people of the Issa Ber. The river is our life. We'll leave the horses and take the river north. We can acquire more when we arrive in Gao."

Changa inspected his steed as he unbridled the beast. It was a fine animal, strong and fearless. He hated leaving it behind but there was no room in a canoe for a horse. He reconsidered when the first canoe was lifted from its hidden pit. They were the largest he'd seen, clearly capable of carrying scores of people and at least three horses. The Songhai unearthed four in all, more than enough to accommodate the Songhai and his crew.

By morning they were prepared to leave. The servants loaded the canoes while Changa and Yusef said their goodbyes.

"Be safe, Kibwana," Yusef said.

"You too, Yusef," Changa struck his arm. "And take care of you wife and children. They are you true treasure."

Yusef smiled. "You take care of Panya. I sense she is not happy about this safari."

"She's not," Changa replied. "She won't say why, but I suspect I'll discover the reason soon enough."

Yusef and his porters departed, taking the route revealed to them by Sibiri. Changa, Panya, Sibiri and the others boarded the canoes and then set off north to Songhai. A journey that would normally have taken weeks overland took only days. They traveled throughout the day, pulling to the banks to eat and to rest during the night. A number of times they took to land to avoid the territorial hippos, but otherwise it was a swift and uneventful journey. Soon they encountered other boats of various sizes on the river, some fishing boats, others moving goods up and down the river to the villages that became more numerous as they drew nearer to Gao. They reached Gao at sunrise, the towers of her mud brick mosques jutting over the dusky horizon. The pale pastels of the Sahel were livened by the colorful clothing of the people. Folk crowded around the riverbank, washing, fishing, hawking and playing. The Issa Ber was the life of Gao and the soul of the Songhai.

The oarsmen guided the canoes to an open space on the crowded bank. A slim bare-chested man ran to them as they moored.

Sibiri was the first to disembark. He said a few words to the man and the man bowed deeply before running off into the city. Changa and the others joined Sibiri.

"My men will unload your goods then store them in my warehouse," he said.

"I hope you don't mind if a few of my baharia accompany them," Changa said.

Sibiri laughed. "Changa Diop! Always the cautious one!"

"Not cautious, just jaded. So when do we meet your employer?"

"Tonight," Sibiri replied. "He is a secretive man. One of his status must be careful."

Once the merchandise was unloaded and secured they proceeded into Gao. Wide dusty streets were bordered by mud brick compounds, the journey often interrupted by markets which increased in size as they work their way closer to the city center. A large mosque occupied the heart of Gao. It towered over the nearby compounds, its magnificence rivaled only by the palace which stood beside it. Sibiri led them to his compound, a spacious areas befitting a successful merchant and a man of lineage. He was greeted by servants and a host of children.

"My servants will show you to your quarters," he said. "I took the liberty of housing you and Panya together. You must tell everyone she is your wife. We are strict in our ways so close to the mosque."

Changa and Panya shared a smile. Changa waved Nafasi over.

"Be sure to be vigilant of our goods and urge the men to stay sharp. I'm still don't fully trust our host."

"Nor do I," Nafasi said. "It will be done, Changa."

Changa and Panya retired to their quarters. A long journey usually ended with them in each others arms but exhaustion and tension set them to sleep alone.

When Changa awoke dusk was upon the city. Panya lay

in her bed fast asleep. A gentle tapping on his door caught his attention. He opened it, revealing a woman wrapped in a plain blue dress and head wrap.

"Master Sibiri summons you," she whispered.

Changa followed the woman to the main building in the compound, Sibiri's home. Sibiri sat under a shade tree opposite a man covered in rich robes, his face obscured by a veil. Two Seljuk bodyguards stood behind the visitor, sabers at their sides, their pale bare arms folded across their chests. The Seljuks studied Changa as he approached, noting the sword at his side. Sibiri smiled then waved Changa to the stool beside him. Changa sat then bowed slightly to the mysterious guest.

"Changa, this is my employer," Sibiri said.

"Does this employer have a name?" Changa said.

The bodyguards were not pleased with Changa's inquiry. They moved closer to the man. He raised his hand and they halted.

"My name is not important," he said.

"It is to me," Changa replied. "A name reveals much of the man."

The man laughed through his veil. "I see. My name is Diallo."

Changa glanced at Sibiri as the man spoke his name. His host's slight grin told him that the stranger was lying.

"So Diallo, Sibiri tells me my so-called talents would be helpful to you."

"Sibiri assures me you have special skills that would be useful to me. I must admit than other being bigger than your average merchant I see none."

"Maybe Sibiri is not as perceptive as he thinks."

Diallo shrugged. "He is an old friend and a trusted… employee. I will take his word despite my doubts."

The man reached into his sleeve then extracted a scroll.

"I take it Sibiri has told you about what I'm seeking and its worth," he said.

Changa nodded as he took the scroll. He unrolled it, revealing a map.

"This map leads to where the book is located."

Changa studied the map intently. This land was totally unfamiliar to him.

"I don't understand," he finally said. "You know what you want and you know where it is. So why ask me to retrieve it?"

"Retrieving the book requires dealing with certain… difficulties. Sibiri tells me you might be able to overcome them."

"Sibiri is optimistic," Changa said.

"I will not play at words with you," Diallo said. "This is a simple decision. Either you will take the job or you won't."

Apparently Diallo was a man not used to being refused, but Changa was a man not used to being pressured.

"I'll require additional payment before we leave," Changa said. "I sustained a substantial loss when we were forced to leave Kanem."

Diallo huffed. "That was not my doing."

"Nevertheless it's what I require," Changa replied.

Diallo nodded. "What else?"

" We'll need provisions for the journey."

"That will be provided. I will also send men to protect you. The desert is a dangerous place."

"I need no protection. I have my men."

Diallo's eyes narrowed. "I insist."

"Two," Changa said.

Diallo leaned back. "Two what?"

"Two of your men, no more," Changa said. "That should be enough to keep an eye on me."

"You push this too far, Changa," Sibiri warned.

"No, Sibiri," Diallo said. "Your friend is cautious. Besides, it's a long way to Mombasa. If he decides to betray us I'm sure we'll meet again before he reaches his destination."

Diallo raised his jeweled hand then snapped his fingers. One of his bodyguards exited the room then returned with a small bag. He dropped it before Changa. Changa opened the bag then grinned. It was filled with gold dust.

"We have a deal, Changa of Mombasa," Diallo said as he stood. "These two will accompany you on your journey. Your supplies and beasts will arrive in the morning. I expect you to be on your way before sunset."

"It may take us more time to prepare," Changa said.

"It won't," Diallo said. "You are under my employ now. You will do as I demand until otherwise."

Changa had to force back a laugh. "As you wish."

Sibiri jumped to his feet. "Master...I mean Diallo. I will send my men to accompany you home."

"Don't bother. It is a cool night and I know the way. Allah be with you, Changa."

Diallo and his escorted departed, Sibiri close on his heels. Changa stood return to his house. As he walked away one of Diallo guards came to him then placed a firm hand on his shoulder.

"We will be watching you, merchant,' he said.

Changa grabbed the man's hand then twisted. The guard dropped to his knees in pain. Before the other guard could react Changa had his shimsar out, its point at his throat.

"Don't underestimate me or my men," Changa replied, his eyes on Diallo. "Many have and now sit with their ancestors. Your master need not worry. I am a man of my word."

He let go of the man hand, sheathed his sword then went to his house. Panya sat on her bed, a distant look in her eyes. He cleared his throat and startled her.

"Changa! How did the meeting go?"

"Well enough." He took off his sword then sat beside her.

"Sibiri's master plays mysterious but he's honest enough beyond lying about his name. If we had more time I'd drop a few coins to find out more about him. He gave me this."

Changa handed her the bag of gold dust. The sight of the pouch brought more tension to her face. Changa noticed then scowled.

"You have been sour ever since we reached Kanem. What is bothering you?"

"I told you before. We are close to my homeland. The memories of my time there are not pleasant."

"It's more than that," he said.

She looked into his eyes, placing the bag of gold dust aside.

"Yes, it is more but I cannot say," she admitted.

Changa pulled her close. "Why?"

"Because I am not sure exactly what it is."

3

THE SAND MEN

Sibiri's compound bustled with the energy of a new adventure. Theirs would be a small caravan but their purpose was not trade. Changa watched from a distance as Sibiri's men and the baharia loaded the camels. He was no stranger to traveling the desert but had no liking of the beasts. He observed them a few moments longer then strolled over to Panya who was inspecting their horses. She greeted him with a skeptical gaze.

"Are you sure about this, Changa?" Panya asked.

"No, but we don't have much choice," he answered.

"We do have a choice. Trading has gone well," she said.

Changa turned to Panya. "Yes, but not well enough."

Panya grabbed his arm. "If you are trying to match what we brought from the east we will be here for a very long time. The goods we trade here are more common, except for those from the east. We have more than enough for the men."

"But not enough for me," he replied. "I need an army, Panya. What we have won't pay for it."

"You don't need as much as you think," she said.

"How do you know?" he said.

Panya glared at him then walked away. Whatever troubled her was beginning to affect him. A shroud of doubt covered this safari. Panya's attitude and the absence of old friends gave this safari a different feel he had yet to get used to.

"Changa Diop!"

Changa turned in the direction of Sibiri's voice and received a shock. The Songhai sauntered toward him accompanied by another man whose appearance brought back a host of hopeful memories. The man was covered with blue robes, a blue turban covering his head, a face veil hiding his mouth and nose. A takouba hung from his shoulder in worn leather baldric. The man stared at Changa intensely. Although he knew it wasn't him, he couldn't help but smile.

"It is a good day to begin a caravan," Sibiri commented.

Changa ignored his words, his attention taken by the man who resembled his long lost friend. "Who is this?"

"This is Athmane. He will be your guide."

"You are Tuareg?"

The man flinched at the word and Sibiri smiled.

"They prefer to be called Ihaggaren," he said. "No one knows the Sahara better than these folks and Athmane is one of the best."

"Welcome to our group," Changa said. The man looked at him warily.

"I will inspect your camels," the man replied. He brushed by Changa.

Sibiri watched him walk away. "They are a difficult lot, these Tuaregs,"

"Not the one I knew," Changa replied. "He was a trusted and loyal friend."

"Really? I doubt it. Keep an eye on this one. Despite his skills, he is still a Tuareg. They are the best guides, but they are fiercely loyal to their own. They are also thieves and caravan raiders."

The two men shared a friendly hug.

"Allah be with you, Changa Diop. May your journey be swift and uneventful."

Changa smirked. "I doubt that it will."

*   *   *

The caravan finally set out at dusk. They journeyed at a leisurely pace, Athmane leading the way with his camel. Changa and Panya walked side by side with their horses.

"He brings back memories," Panya said.

"Yes he does," Changa replied. "Good and bad. Mostly good, though. Sibiri says we should keep a close eye on him. What do you sense?"

"He seems an honest man, but his loyalties are not with the Songhai. I don't think he means us harm."

For three days they kept the same routine, traveling through the night and hiding from the intense sun during the day. On the fourth day Changa was surprised to find Athmane walking beside him.

"You know my people," Athmane said.

"No, I knew one of your people," Changa answered. "He was a very good friend."

"What was his name?"

Changa frowned. "I don't know. He never told me. He took a vow of silence before we met. We called him Tuareg."

Athmane flinched. "Is he dead?"

"No, at least I don't think so. We lost him in Mogadishu. He saved our lives."

"He was surely Ihaggaren," Athmane said. "Only a true warrior would give his life for his friends."

Changa didn't reply. He would not give up hope that his friend was alive.

"Why do you take this journey?" Athmane asked.

"Diallo pays a good price," Changa replied. "And I am a man in need of gold."

Athmane looked away. "I do not know this Diallo. If he is Songhai, he is untrustworthy."

"Sibiri says the same of you."

Athmane spit. "Sibiri is a camel's ass."

"Yet you work for him."

Athmane looked at Changa, his eyes smiling. "I am a man in need of gold..."

They shared a hearty laugh.

"Tell me, Changa of Mombasa, why do you think this Diallo chose you for this task?"

"According to Sibiri he was impressed by my skills."

Athmane gazed toward the hidden horizon. "Did you wonder why he could not trust one of his own to make this journey?"

"Actually, I didn't."

"It is because none would accept it," Athmane replied. "At any price."

"What are you saying, Athmane?"

"Just a warning, Changa of Mombasa. I can take you anywhere you wish to go. There are other cities where you can trade your way to wealth."

"I have a deal with Diallo," Changa replied. "I am a man of my word."

"Then I shall take you where you wish to go," Athmane answered. "I will speak no more of this. Allah be with you."

Athmane picked up his pace, taking the lead of the caravan. As the sun rose over the dunes they bedded down again but Changa could not sleep. He began to wonder why Diallo and Sibiri chose him for the task. A grin slowly formed on his face; Sibiri appealed to his vanity and Diallo appealed to his greed. Memories of Zheng San and the Malaccan Strait came to mind. This was a dangerous task apparently, as to what danger he could not guess. But there was nothing he could do at this point. He'd given his word and he needed the gold.

"Changa! Changa!"

Changa jumped to his feet as he grabbed his weapons. Panya came to his side, whip and sword in hand. Nafasi and the other baharia stood as well, all of them looking toward a towering dune to the east. Figures crested the hill, their details indistinguishable from the distance. But a sickening stirring in Changa's gut told him what was occurring.

Panya grabbed his arm. "Tebo?"

Changa nodded. "It seems I will never escape Usenge's reach."

He gripped his throwing knifes in his hands then marched toward the advancing figures. The baharia looked at him helplessly, knowing that this was a fight they could not support. Athmane gazed at him in interest; Diallo's Seljuks extracted their scimitars and came to his side.

"You can't help me," Changa said.

"Our master commanded us to stay with you," one of the Seljuks answered.

Changa studied them both then shrugged.

"Follow at your own risk," he said.

The three advanced on the approaching shapes. As they neared the Seljuks faltered for a moment and Changa grinned. The tebos never ceased to amaze him in the shapes they took. The figures were shaped like men but were featureless. They were formed completely of sand. Their size was not intimidating. It was the number of them, at least twenty in all.

"Allah Akbar!" The Seljuks charged by him, scimitars raised over their heads. The sandmen didn't resist the bodyguards' attack. Their blades cut through the sandmen like air but the creatures did not falter. One of the sandmen drew back its fist then slammed it into a Seljuk's chest, knocking the hapless man into the air. He landed at Changa's feet, his chest crushed. Changa jumped over the dead man, rushing to save his comrade. A sand man gripped the other Seljuk's neck then lifted him off his feet. Changa threw his knife. The blade sank into the sand man's body and it disintegrated into a pile of sand. The Seljuk fell atop the mass gasping. To his terror the sand slithered around him, working its way to the remaining sandmen. The creatures' size increased slightly.

The Seljuk clambered to his feet then fled.

"This is Shatain's work!" he shouted. "You are cursed!"

"Not exactly," Changa said under his breath. He ran to retrieve his knife as the others sandmen converged on him. He counted his knives and the number of advancing sandmen. There were more sandmen than knives. This was not good.

He heard sand crunching behind him then spun, a knife ready to throw. Nafasi and Panya stood ready, weapons in hand.

"Go back," he said. "You know you cannot harm them."

"I can delay them," Panya said.

"And I can help you throw," Nafasi said.

Changa tossed two throwing knives to Nafasi as Panya reached into her bag then extracted a combination of colorful powders. She tossed the powder into the air as she whispered into the sky; a strong wind stirred behind her. She looked at Changa and Nafasi.

"It will not destroy them, but it will slow them down."

She swept her arms forward and the wind rushed by them. It slammed into the animated sand like a wall, sending them stumbling backwards but only for a moment. They continued trudging through the gale, their progress slowed.

"It doesn't matter where you hit them," Changa said to Nafasi. "As long as you hit them. Don't waste my knives!"

"I won't Changa," Nafasi said. "I promise."

They split, Changa jogging right, Nafasi left. It was Changa who the sandmen sought so they followed him as he moved; freeing Nafasi to take his time. His hours of practice proved fruitful. He struck down the sandmen one by one as Changa dealt with them face to face. The fewer the tebo, the larger they became and the longer for the knives to have an effect. Finally one large sandman loomed before Changa, its size and strength allowing it to move faster against Panya's windy onslaught.

"We must throw together!" Changa shouted to Nafasi.

Nafasi nodded. They both held knives in each hand,

advancing toward the hulking creature.

"Now!" Changa shouted.

Four iron throwing knives cut through the air then sank into the massive sand tebo. The creature shuddered; a deep moan vibrated through the sand as Panya's wind etched the creature away until it stood no higher than Changa. The pile dissipated and a stabbing pain passed through Changa. He heard his name on the wind as he fell to his knees, grasping his chest. The sensation slowly subsided as Panya ran through the sand to his side.

"Changa! Are you alright?"

"No." He collapsed into the sand, still clutching his chest. Darkness engulfed him then transmuted into dense trees. The air became humid around him; he blinked his eyes and an ominous masked face filled his view.

"Usenge," he croaked.

"Son of Mfumu,' the masked face answered. "You have come too close. I have you in my hands now."

Pain erupted in Changa's chest.

"I could kill you here," Usenge said. "But my people must see you die, just like they saw your father. They must know that Mfumu's seed is no more. Then they will…"

Usenge's image distorted, swirling before Changa like windblown sand. The trees wavered until the darkness gripped him again. The cool humid air was replaced by arid desert heat and intense light. Changa shielded his eyes from the sunlight. He felt an object on his chest then reached for it. It was a throwing knife. He shifted his head to the right and saw Panya's relieved face, her lips moving in a whispered chant. The baharia surrounded him; they cheered when he sat upright, the knife falling into his hands. Panya hugged him and cried.

"You were lost to me," she sobbed.

Changa didn't answer. He dropped the knife into the sand, eased his arms around her then pulled her tight.

*   *   *

Another pair of eyes studied Changa, filled with confirmation. Athmane turned away as the outlanders celebrated their leader's return from the dead. He went to the body of the dead Seljuk then spat on it. The other Seljuk sat nearby, watching Changa and the others as he nursed his throat. Athmane pulled a dagger from his waist belt then slashed the bodyguard's neck from behind. The man stiffened then fell forward. Satisfied with his work, he mounted his camel then rode away, disappearing over the horizon.

4

EL SIROCCO

Sibiri told Changa not to trust the Tuareg. Apparently he was right. It was almost nightfall when Nafasi noticed Athmane was missing. It took another two hours of searching and waiting before they realized he was not returning. Changa was still weak from his ordeal with the sand men but decisions needed to be made quickly.

Panya followed him as he left his tent to meet with Nafasi. The young navigator was inspecting provisions when Changa approached him.

"Did he take anything?" Changa asked.

"No," Nafasi replied. "He killed the Seljuk then slipped away."

"Why would he kill the bodyguard?" Panya asked.

"There is no love lost between the Tuaregs and the Songhai," Changa answered. "The Seljuks were Diallo's servants."

"But why would he leave us here?" Nafasi asked.

"We work for the Songhai," Changa answered. "And our encounter with the tebo may have shaken him as well. But there is nothing we can do about that. He's gone. The biggest question is how do we continue without him?"

"We have the map," Nafasi said. "And I am a decent navigator."

"You are more than decent," Changa replied. "But I don't see how navigating will help us here."

"The desert is but a sea with sand," Nafasi answered. "I have plotted our course as we traveled. The stars are the same in most cases and north is always north. I'm assuming we traveled in a fairly straight direction since there are few obstacles save the dunes. I can get us to our destination. The question is should we continue."

"We need water," Panya commented.

"And Athmane knew where to find it," Changa said.

"We know where the wells are behind us, but not before us," Nafasi said.

"Then we have no choice," Changa said. "We must go back."

Changa folded his arms across his chest. Once again he thought this safari had been a bad idea.

"Tell the men," he said. "We head back to Gao."

He was walking back to his tent when high pitched ululations shattered the silence. Camel riders broke the horizon as they crested the dunes, followed by men running on foot with shields and spears. All were clad in blue robes of various shades, their faces hidden.

"Baharia!" Changa shouted.

His men responded. In moments they formed a circle in the middle of the camp, the horses and camels in the center. They raised their bows, ready to repeal the coming attack. The blue ring halted outside of arrow range; only two riders continued to advance. One of the Tuaregs rode a towering white camel, the beast festooned in gold trappings and bright green tassels. As they came closer Changa recognized the other rider as Athmane.

"The betrayer has returned," Changa whispered. "Panya, come with me. It seems we are to negotiate our freedom."

Changa and Panya mounted their horses then rode from the circle towards the advancing duo. The camel riders halted; their camels knelt and the men dismounted. Changa and Panya dismounted as well. As they marched through the sand Changa's attention was taken by the other man. It was his walk he noticed first, strong, forceful and familiar. Then his weapons; a takouba hung from his shoulders in a worn baldric, a scimitar tucked in his sash. Changa's pace quickened as did the man's. In moments they were running toward each other, Changa's eyes filled with joyful tears. The men hugged, beating each other's backs.

"Tuareg!" Changa shouted.

"Changa, my brother!" the man replied.

Changa shoved his old friend away, stunned. He spoke! He laughed and they hugged again. Athmane looked on with bright eyes.

"Tuareg!" Panya cried.

Changa stepped aside and Panya jumped into the Tuareg's arms.

"Lady Panya," the Tuareg said in a deep, resonant voice. "Tinariwen is blessed with your beauty."

Panya pulled back, shock on her face.

"Finally! It is a voice befitting the man."

By the time the Tuareg put Panya down the baharia were running to the trio, their voices filled with celebration. The Tuareg's men relaxed, their camels kneeling into the soft sand. Those on foot leaned on their spears and shields.

"You survived Mogadishu," Changa said, stating the obvious.

"Mogadishu was the least of my worries," he replied. "The journey home was much more interesting. But Allah protected me, and now I know why."

Changa turned to Athmane. "You knew."

"I suspected," Athmane replied. "I volunteered to be your guide when I heard Sibiri speak your name. Akedamel Sirocco speaks often of you and your baharia."

"Akedamel Sirocco?" Changa smiled. "So not only do you speak, you have a name."

The Tuareg laughed. "Akedamel is a title; Sirocco is my calling. It means the Desert Wind. My true name is Warani."

Changa stepped aside as the baharia swarmed Warani.

A song broke out among them; some of them danced. Changa looked at his old friend with joy.

"If I never make another trade on this safari it wouldn't matter. I've found my brother again."

Warani worked his way to Changa and Panya.

"Come with us. We have a camp not far from here. You will eat, rest then we will discuss your journey."

The caravan headed west, finally arriving at a large oasis nestled in a deep valley. Ululations greeted them as they entered, women and children surrounding Changa, Panya and the baharia. They clapped their hands as they followed the baharia to Warani's tent. Servants bringing food and drink followed them inside the grandiose shelter. Wide Persian carpets covered the sand with large silk resting pillows surrounding low serving tables. Piles of riches bordered the edge of the sitting area. Warani sat at the largest table in the center of the tent then gestured for Changa, Panya and Nafasi to sit as well. Nafasi seemed stunned by his invitation to the circle. Panya patted his shoulder then shared a smile.

"You are our navigator now," she said. "You must get used to this."

The trio joined their friend as the servants served the meal.

"So Changa, we must discuss this safari," Warani said.

"Not before you tell us how you came to be here," Changa replied.

"I have come full circle," Warani said. "Before our meeting Tinariwen was my home. Then I was known as El Sirocco but I was a different man, a cruel. Some would say an evil man."

Warani shifted his alasho then took a sip of water from a golden goblet.

"Then Allah intervened. I was seduced by the daughter of a witch I sentenced to death. She condemned me to a fate worse than death for an Imajaghan, the life of a slave. I thought of fighting, of attempting to free myself, but during my journey to captivity I wondered about on the man I was then decided to accept Allah's will. My master quickly learned I was not one for hard labor, so he decided to use me for what our men are known best."

"A fighter," Changa answered.

Warani nodded. "This is how you came to find me in the pits of Mogadishu."

Nafasi bit into a flank of lamb then washed it down with palm wine before speaking.

"Bwana Warani, you were a pit fighter?"

"Yes I was, and to you it is just Warani."

"I travelled to Mogadishu to re-establish trade with clients of Belay after his death," Changa said. "One of them, Kabili, insisted I enjoy an evening at the pits despite knowing I once fought in them. On the day I attended the Tuareg, I mean Warani, was fighting, but I discovered his match was a death sentence. His master had tired of him and decided to have him fight until he was killed. I could not tolerate it, so I assisted him."

Warani laughed. "You did more than assist me. You saved my life."

"And you have returned the favor a thousand times," Changa answered. "I still don't understand why you insisted to serve with me after I gave you your freedom."

"It was Allah's will," Warani replied. "If I had not I would not be the man I am today. You taught me how to be a good leader. You taught me how to care about those who serve me."

It was Changa's turn to laugh. "No one here serves me. We are a family."

Warani nodded. "Exactly."

Warani placed down his goblet. "My return was not well received. I made many enemies long ago and they all greeted me as enemies are prone to do."

"No one ever believed you were dead," Athmane said. "People thought Death feared if it tried to kill you and failed you would make it suffer most horribly."

Warani laughed. "I sought no honor and no position when I returned, but many who had followed me before wished to do so again. So I formed my kel."

Warani took another sip of water. "Now we must discuss your safari. You are my brother, Changa, so take my words seriously. Do not go to the oasis."

Changa was familiar with the look in Warani's eyes. It was a warning.

"I cannot break a deal," Changa said. "I have to go."

"Your reputation is well known among the Swahili and beyond," Warani replied. "No one knows you here. You can return east and no one will know better or think any less of you."

"I will know," Changa said. "Now tell me why I should not go."

"This Diallo chose you because no one in Songhai or Tinariwen will accept his charge. That place is cursed. My people call it Paradise."

Changa grinned. "A lovely name for such a dangerous place."

"We call it such because those who enter never return," Athmane said. "It's like entering Heaven…or Hell."

"Still, I must go," Changa said. "Like I said before, I've given my word and accepted payment."

"I insist you not go, Changa," Warani said. His voice was forceful, almost commanding.

"I'm going," Changa answered.

The two stared at each other, an unspoken discussion passing between them.

Warani's shoulders slumped. "Then I have no choice. We will go with you."

"Didn't you just try to warn me to stay away?" Changa said.

Warani's eyes brightened. "Yes. But you are my brother

and I go where you go. Besides, someone will need to be there to save you."

"I'm not sure he will need us," Athmane said. "I saw him fight the sand men."

"He will," Warani replied. "Changa has a tendency to draw danger."

A knowing look passed between the old friends.

"Then it is settled," Changa said. "With your permission we'll set out in the morning."

"It will be good to have you with us again," Panya said.

Warani's eyes went serious.

"Let's hope it won't be fatal."

5

PARADISE

The oasis rested in a shallow valley walled by a crescent of low dunes to the north. Towering desert palms peered from the dense foliage like sentinels scrutinizing the surrounding sands. A temperate breeze hissed through the undergrowth, a soothing sound that reached the ears of the baharia and Ihaggaren staring from a distance.

Changa's horse fidgeted under him, clearly disturbed. Panya looked at the oasis then to Changa, her face lined with worry. Warani kept his eyes on the oasis and his hands on his swords.

"I ask you one more time, brother. Do not do this," he said.

Changa didn't reply. He was so close to heeding Warani's advice. There was something about the oasis that hinted at danger, but at the same time something compelling that reached into his mind then beckoned him forward.

"I agree with Warani," Panya said. "There are spirits here, ancient ones."

"Good or bad?" Changa asked.

"Those terms don't apply to spirits," Panya answered. "You know this."

Changa rubbed his chin. Diallo promised him a fortune if he returned with the book. The mysterious merchant proved capable of fulfilling that promise. Yet he was not one to risk his life unnecessarily.

"You may be right, Warani," he finally said. "Some rewards

are not worth the price. Let's…"

A roar burst from beyond the oasis. The dunes melted into a raging twister of sand then surged toward them with striking swiftness. Before they could flee the sudden sandstorm engulfed them. Baharia and Ihaggaren yelled and cursed as the stinging sand shoved them about and tumbled them off their horses and camels. Everyone except Changa. A force gripped him like an invisible hand, jerking him from his horse then dragging him toward the oasis, his toes barely touching the sand. Changa strained his massive muscles against the force to no avail. The winds diminished as he neared the oasis; the force relenting as he was pulled into the woods. He stumbled then fell onto his chest. Something crunched under him and he quickly rolled up then looked down. He stood on broken human bones. Changa considered his situation. Behind him the sandstorm raged, the oasis shielded from its fury by an unseen barrier. The rustling of leaves caught his attention; as he gripped his shimsar hilt the vegetation before him shifted, clearing a path to a modest stone building in the distance. Changa looked at the building then to the furious storm behind him. He decided to take his chances in the storm.

He strode to the oasis edge, tying an alasho around his nose and mouth. He stepped to the sand but struck an invisible barrier. He pushed at it with his hand; the blockade stretched but would not let him through. Changa took out his sword, striking the barrier with all his strength but it would not give. Exasperated, he looked back at the temple.

"It seems I have no choice," he said.

Changa walked slowly to the structure, studying his surroundings as he approached. The oasis was a graveyard, the final resting place for the hundreds, maybe thousands who had most likely come to claim the book. The morbid scene did little to encourage him. As he came closer the bones seemed more recent. Fabric and armor draped from the remains, some he recognized,

Changa came forward, his sword at guard.

"Put that down," the guardian said. "You have proven yourself. But I sense the book is not meant for you."

Changa raised his sword again. "I've been sent to claim it."

The guardian leaned toward Changa. "Who sent you?"

"Diallo."

The guardian nodded. "A clever name. Maybe he is worthy after all."

The guardian placed his sword and pipe aside then held out his hands. Haze from the room gathered over his palms as he chanted in a language Changa did not recognize. A shape formed over his palms, becoming more defined as the guardian's form dissipated.

"Tell Diallo the legacy has been passed to him," the guardian said. "The Nyama Book is his. Sumunguru has decreed it so."

The guardian disappeared. The book hung in the air for a moment then fell. Changa dropped his sword then lunged for it, wincing as he caught it. The light surrounding him increased; he looked up to discover he was outside. The temple was gone, as was the storm. Changa's wound ached; he looked down to see the blood flowing from it again. He tucked the book under his arm then pressed the cut with his free hand. Taking a deep breath he stumbled for the edge of the oasis.

The ground shook. Changa looked down just a skeletal hand burst from the sand then grabbed his ankle. He pulled his leg free just as another hand came forth then grabbed his thigh. Changa twisted free then ran for the desert. A macabre scene surrounded him; dead warriors rising from the sand, their mishappend arms reaching for the prize he carried. Changa swung wildly with his blade, clutching the book close to his chest. With each swing he weakened, Sumunguru's wound taking its toll. He fell to his knees, gritting his teeth as he battled the undead assault.

As he neared the limits of his strenght he heard his name.

"Changa! Changa!"

A gap opened before him. Warani appeared, whirling with both blades, striking down dead warriors a second time. Panya was close behind, shattering bones with her whip and machete. Baharia and Ihaggaren rushed from behind them, forming a protective shield around Changa.

Nafasi grabbed Changa's arm then lifted him to his feet. I have him!" Nafasi shouted.

Warani and Panya formed the vanguard as they cut their way through the dead toward the desert. Changa stumbled with Nafasi, fighting hard to stay conscious. As they cleared the foliage the eerie pursuit ended. The dead returned to their graves, the Nyama Book once again escaping their grasp.

Changa and Nafasi collapsed, both men panting. Changa looked to his wound; his left side was soaked with blood. Warani dropped to his knees before him, his eyes fixed on Changa's wound. Panya shoved the Ihaggaren aside. She pulled up Changa's shirt and mail to look at his wound. After a swift assessment she opened her pouch then went to work. Warani's eyes drifted to the book.

"So you have it."

Changa nodded, too weak to speak.

Warani frowned, stood, then turned and walked away.

"He's not happy," Panya commented.

"I did what I was paid to do," Changa replied.

"Be quiet," Panya said. "Let's save your life first. Then we'll deal with Warani."

6

A MEETING IN TIMBUKTU

Changa sat with his arms crossed, the scowl on his face a reflection of his mood. Warani took the same pose, his eyes narrowed as he looked at his friend. His men stood behind him, their postures threatening. The baharia backed Changa, their stances just as tense.

"You're asking me to break my word," Changa said.

"I'm asking you to trust me, my brother," Warani replied.

"Diallo trusts me to bring the book to him. He paid me," Changa said

"That is what this is all about," Warani said. "You have a bond sealed with gold. What you possess transcends any payment. It could mean the end of my people."

"You exaggerate," Changa said.

"Do I? I don't know who this Diallo is, but I do know the Songhai despise us. We have fought them and kept them at bay for generations. But what you possess could change our fortune."

"You make assumptions," Changa said. "Diallo may have nothing to do with the Songhai."

"Changa, listen to him," Panya said. "He is our brother. Don't let your greed blind you reason."

Changa jerked his head toward Panya. Her words angered him because they were true.

"So what do you propose?" Changa asked. "All this effort will not go to waste."

Warani's eyes smiled. "There is a man in Timbuktu. He will be very interested in this book."

"And how do I know he will use this book in the proper way?"

"Because he is Ihaggaren," Warani answered. "I know him well and he is a good man. He is also a good Muslim. He would never use such power."

"We owe the Songhai nothing," Nafasi said. "Once we sell the book we will be gone from here."

It was obvious the baharia did not want to fight Warani and his warriors. Changa shrugged then sighed.

"We will go to Timbuktu," he said. "If your friend's offer is not satisfactory I will take the book to Diallo."

"So be it," Warani said. He turned to him men. "So be it."

They broke camp soon afterwards, the baharia following the Ihaggaren south to Timbuktu. Changa's mood was mixed throughout the journey. He was not a man to break his word, but Warani was his friend and would not steer him wrong. Still, it was not his way. The other reason for his mood was the fact that both Panya and Nafasi disagreed with him. That was unexpected. He wasn't surprised by Warani; he looked out for his people as he should. But disagreement from his own? It was a sign that this safari had gone long enough. He hoped the man in Timbuktu offered enough gold to bring it to an end.

Timbuktu rose gradually over the horizon, a sprawling city of bi-level mud brick homes and towering mosques. The reputation of the city reached the Swahili Coast for it was a city of higher education and vast libraries. It was also a trading city, which interested Changa the most. As they reached the city's outskirts Changa worked his mount close to Warani.

"So where will we find this friend of yours?"

Warani laughed. "You do not trust me, brother?"

"You are a leader of men," Changa answered. "You will do

what you must to protect your people."

Warani nodded. "That's true, but I would never lie to you, Changa. You are my brother. It is because of you that I am the leader I am now."

Changa felt embarrassed doubting Warani.

"Lead the way," he finally said. "This book is becoming a burden."

They travelled the wide avenues to the city center, passing through the main market before Warani raised his hand for everyone to stop.

"There," he said, pointing to a squat building near the largest mosque. A young boy in a dingy robe stood beside the door, his attention focused on the dusty leather bound book in his hands. Warani and Changa were almost upon him before he jerked up his head.

"Oh…greetings elders," he stuttered. "How can I serve you?"

"We are here to see Saabir ibn Rasheed," Warani said.

The boy closed the book, tucked it under his arm then bowed. "The master is inside. Come with me."

The boy pushed opened the thick doors with his free hand. Cool air rushed out to meet them as they entered the dimly lit building. Changa smiled as he entered, immediately impressed by the massive library. Shelves of books and scrolls scaled every wall. Between the shelves robed men sat at low tables with candles, straining their eyes as they studied the texts before them. A thin man emerged from behind the counter before them, dressed similar to Warani but with less accoutrements. A thick beard covered his slim unveiled face, his smile barely visible. He looked briefly at Changa and Warani before the leather satchel hanging from Changa's shoulder caught his attention.

"Welcome El Sirocco," he said in a soft voice. "It has been a long time."

"Too long Saabir," Warani replied.

Changa cleared his throat. He was not here to socialize.

"This is my brother Changa Diop. He has something he wishes to sell."

"Something I might wish to sell," Changa corrected him.

Saabir looked at Changa with curious eyes. "Follow me."

They walked to the counter at the rear of the library. Changa placed the satchel on the counter then took out the book. Saabir gasped, grasping his chest as he stumbled back.

"This is not real!" he said. He hurried from the counter.

"Out, out! Everyone out!"

He scurried from table to table, pushing folks from their seats.

"Baizeed! Help me!" he called out.

The door opened then the boy entered. He looked at Saabir wide eyed then repeated his actions, running from table to table, forcing the patrons out the door. He followed the last person out then closed the door behind him.

Saabir returned to the counter winded.

"Do you know what you possess?" he stammered.

"I believe I do," Changa replied. "It was given to me by Sumunguru."

Saabir gripped his chest again. "You saw him? You spoke to him? You're still alive?"

"Changa is a man with unique abilities," Warani said.

"You have done the right thing bringing the book here," Saabir said. "We will make sure it is never found again!"

Saabir reached for the book. Changa placed his hand on it.

"This is not a gift, Saabir," he said.

The librarian looked surprised. His eyes went to Warani.

"Changa was offered a great deal of gold to deliver this book to a buyer in Gao. I had to persuade him to come here."

"You can't put a value on something like this!" Saabir

said.

"You can't but I can," Changa replied. "This book remains with me until I'm paid."

Saabir glared at Warani. "You will allow this?"

"It is the honorable thing to do, my friend," Warani answered.

"There is no honor in this!" Saabir shouted.

Changa took the book from the counter.

"This was a waste of time," he said.

"No, wait!" Saabir rubbed his forehead. "I'll pay your price."

Changa's eyes narrowed as he suppressed a grin. "You don't know my price."

"It doesn't matter. I'll pay it."

Changa folded his arms across his chest. "Two bags of gold dust."

Both Saabir and Warani gasped.

"You didn't bring me a merchant. You brought me a robber!" Saabir complained. "Still, I will pay. I'll need a few days to raise such a large amount."

"You have three," Changa said. He walked away, Warani following.

"Only an infidel would sell such a book," Saabir called out.

"Then an infidel I am," Changa called back.

Baizeed opened the door for them and they stepped back into the bright afternoon sun.

"Saabir is not rich but he is a very influential man," Warani said. "He will get the gold. I advise we leave as soon as you're paid. You will not be well liked here once the word spreads among certain circles. There is no such thing as a secret in Timbuktu."

"I guess we should camp outside the city?" Changa asked.

"It would be wise," Warani said.

"Still, I would like to explore it," Changa said. "Timbuktu is known throughout the world. I'd like to see why."

The baharia and the Ihaggaren made camp on the city's edge. Changa and his men took in the grand city as they waited for Saabir to collect the gold he promised. Three days after their first meeting the boy Baizeed appeared at their camp riding a donkey.

"Master Diop!" he shouted. "Master Saabir asks for your presence at his library!"

Changa emerged from his tent, Panya at his side.

"So you'll get your gold after all," Panya said.

Changa answered with a smile and a kiss on her cheek.

"I never doubted it."

Panya shoved him away. "Yes you did."

"I would have marched into his library with a torch," Changa said.

"You are a cruel man sometimes, Changa Diop."

Changa grinned. "Only when it comes to gold."

Changa waved Nafasi to him.

"Break camp. Everyone will come with us. We're leaving Timbuktu as soon as we're paid for the book."

"We're going home?" Nafasi asked.

"Yes, my brother. We're going home."

A smile broke across Nafasi's face. He ran to the baharia, spurring everyone along. Warani came to them both, his eyes serious.

"I'm sorry your time here was not more restful," he said. "I'm also sorry you are leaving so soon."

"Had all worked out we would never have come," Changa replied. "But we did get to see you again. The challenges were worth it."

The Ihaggaren and baharia formed a large procession to Saabir's library, led by Baizeed and his donkey. They gathered before the entrance as Changa, Panya and Warani entered. Saabir stood behind the counter, his hands resting on two leather bags. Changa grinned.

"I have your gold," Saabir said.

"You are a man of your word," Changa said.

"Are you a man of yours?" Saabir asked.

Changa placed the satchel containing the book on the counter. Panya took the gold bags; Saabir took the book satchel.

"Allah be with you," Saabir said.

Changa nodded again. "And with you."

They were walking toward the library door when it swung open. Sounds of chaos burst in with Nafasi.

"Changa! The city is under attack!"

Changa and the others ran outside. People darted through the streets, some into their compounds and homes, others toward the desert. Warani unsheathed his swords and did his men. Athmane approached him.

"Songhai," Athmane said calmly. "They came from the river in their damn war canoes. Thousands of them."

"We must go. Hurry!"

The Ihaggaren and baharia were about to mount their beasts when the crowds heading toward the desert ran back toward the city center, pursued by Songhai cavalry striking down people with their sabers. Warani and his men climbed onto their camels then rode through the fleeing town folk, meeting the Songhai cavalry blade to blade.

The baharia looked at Changa, who shrugged then climbed onto his horse. They joined the Ihaggaren and together they beat back the Songhai riders to the city's edge. Their victory was short-lived; Changa looked beyond the fleeing Songhai to another wave of cavalry and infantry emerging from the sands.

"Into the library!" Changa shouted. It was a desperate move. Changa hoped the wave of warriors would sweep by allowing them a moment of confusion to escape. He was not one to run from a fight, but knew when the odds were against him.

The desperate merchants rode back into the city then rushed into the library. Saabir stood behind the counter, clutching his recent purchase against his chest. Baizeed projected a brave image, clutching a dagger as he stood beside his patron, a determined look on his face. The Ihaggaren and baharia drew their weapons, Changa, Warani, Panya and Nafasi standing before them. Sounds of chaos echoed through the library then slowly subsided. The room fell silent save for the desperate breathing of those inside.

"I think the worse has passed," Nafasi said.

The library door burst open. Songhai warriors poured into the room, bows raised, lances lowered. Changa and Warani raised their hands to stay their men response. This was not the time to fight. The Songhai did not immediately attack them, so they would not provoke them. Instead they forced Changa and his companions to the rear of the library.

"Make way!" a heavy voice shouted.

The Songhai warriors parted. Heavily armored warriors armed with long bows entered, parting right and left. A man covered in chain mail and wearing a metal conical cap stepped into the center.

"This way," he ordered.

Changa's group followed the man out of the library then into the streets. The once vibrant thoroughfares were littered with dead bodies and teemed with Songhai warriors. Before them was a pedestal occupied by a large golden throne. The man sitting on the chair was draped in brightly colored robes, his head crowned by a golden cap. A servant stood beside him holding a large blue umbrella trimmed in golden thread. The man on the throne stared at Changa with familiarity in his eyes as he stroked his beard.

"Changa Diop," he said. "We meet again, although I must say I am surprised by the circumstances."

Changa was dumbfounded. "With all respect, I do not know you. I'm a visitor to this land. I am not familiar with

Songhai warriors."

"This is no warrior," Warani said. "This is Sonni Ali, sultan of Songhai."

Changa's eyes widened. This was bad.

"Quiet, Tuareg,'" Sonni Ali said. He turned his attention back to Changa.

"We had a deal, Changa. It seems you broke it."

A chill went through Changa.

"You are Diallo?" Bad had just gone to worse.

Sonni Ali smiled. "I find it prudent to take on a disguise when I move among my people. It is safer that way."

He looked over the others to the rear, his eyes settling on Saabir.

"Bring the librarian to me."

Two warriors dragged Saabir before Sonni Ali, the librarian clutching the satchel to his chest. A tall warrior standing beside the sultan approached the defiant man.

"Give me the book," the warrior ordered.

The librarian turned away, his grip tight on the satchel.

"You must decide what is more important," Sonni Ali said. "Your pride or your life."

The warrior drew his saber. The librarian looked at the gleaming blade then handed the satchel over to the warrior. The warrior took the satchel then stabbed Saabir. Panya rushed to the man's side.

The warrior carried the satchel to Ali. The sultan opened the satchel then smiled. He removed the Nyama Book then placed it gently onto his lap. His fingers shook as he opened it then waved his palm over the page. The papers glowed with a blue green light that drifted into Ali's palm. Ali smiled then looked at Changa, his eyes tinted by the Nyama Book's power.

"You did it," he said to Changa. "I'm very impressed."

He closed the book then placed it back into the satchel. "I'm going to assume you were in Timbuktu for a respite and brought the book to the library for safekeeping on your way to Gao. I'm also going to assume that these Tuaregs came to rob you of the book, and that my journey to Timbuktu just happened to be a fortuitous intervention. I'll assume this so I won't have to kill you. I like you, Changa Diop, and the fact that I have the book tells me that the ancestors favor you as well."

Changa said nothing; there was nothing for him to say.

"I am also going to assume that you brought me this other gift as well." Ali turned his attention to Warani.

"Long have I wished to have the infamous El Sirocco in my grasp. It seems Allah blesses me this day."

The Songhai warriors rushed the Ihaggaren. They disarmed the desert men then tied their hands. As they approached Warani Changa, Panya and Nafasi stood before him.

"Wait," Changa said. "You have assumed much in my favor. Assume also that you owe me the remainder of my payment. Give me El Sirocco and his men."

Sonni Ali laughed. "You are a bold man, Changa Diop. What is this goat worth to you?"

"He is my brother," Changa replied.

Sonny Ali raised his fly whisk. Two burly men struggled with a chest, shuffling before Changa then dropping it before him.

"There was to be two of them," Ali said. "Your Tuaregs will cost you the other."

Two of Changa's baharia came forward to claim the chest. By Changa's estimate his safari had just paid for itself.

"One more thing, Changa," Ali said. "The guardian of the book; did he share words with you?"

"He praised you as a leader," Changa said. "He said you did well by choosing me."

A curious look commanded Ali's face.

"Did he give his name?" he asked.

Changa nodded. "Sumunguru."

Sonni Ali's eyes widened as he sat up on his throne. He raised his fly whisk and the servants sat the other chest before Changa. A third servant approached Changa then hung a solid gold square from his neck inscribed in Arabic.

"Go, Changa Diop. Take your Tuareg friends with you. You have free passage through Songhai. The necklace you wear indicates to everyone in my realm that you are favored by Sonni Ali...and Sumunguru."

Changa bowed, as did the baharia. Ali's men reluctantly freed the Ihaggaren.

'Thank you, Sonni Ali."

Sonni Ali nodded. "You are a special man, Changa Diop. Next time be more prudent in your dealings. It might save your life."

Changa and Ali shared a grin.

Warani and his men led them out of the city through a tight gauntlet of Songhai warriors. The Ihaggaren and Songhai shared hateful stares but discipline ruled over emotions. They remained in tense silence until Timbuktu disappeared behind them.

Changa took a deep breath as they stopped.

"Remind me never to listen to you again," he said to Warani.

"I apologize, my brother," Warani said. "Apparently Sonni Ali does see all."

"It seems you owe me your life again," Changa commented.

"It is yours to command."

Changa laughed. "I believe your men would have something to say about it."

Changa waved to Nafasi. "Bring me the librarian's gold."

The navigator trotted to him with the satchels.

"Can you see that Saabir's family gets this?" Changa asked.

"Of course."

"Bring me one of the chests!"

Three baharia struggled forward with the chest.

"Take this," Changa said. "For your troubles."

Warani raised his hand. "No Changa. I can never repay you for what you've done for me. I am a better man because of it."

They hugged like the old days, pounding each other on the back with blows that would fell lesser men. Warani's eyes glistened as they pulled away. The others fell in line as they hugged their old friend.

"So where do you go now, my brother?" Warani asked.

"Back to Sofala," Changa replied. "I must take my brothers home. They have followed me too long."

Panya approached Warani again. She pulled down his shesh then kissed his cheek.

"Be well, Warani. I will miss you."

"Now this is a proper goodbye," Warani said. "I will miss you too, Panya."

The Ihaggaren and baharia parted ways. Changa looked back, watching Warani for a moment before turning his eyes south. He was losing his brother again. But this time, he was content.

Kitabu ChaTisa

(Book Nine)

A Daughter Returns

1

THE HERB MERCHANT

Panya strolled through the Gao main market, swaying between carts crammed with herbs, plants and spices. A large woven basket dangled from her right arm, the jangling bracelets on her left wrist adding their song to the market din. A simple green dress fell loosely from her shoulders to her sandals, her yellow robe hiding her whip and sword. A thin headscarf covered her braided hair while large golden earrings swayed with each step. She walked among the merchants and buyers alone, grateful to be away from her brother baharias' overbearing attention and Changa's constant questions. True, she had not been herself lately, but not for the reasons they suspected.

She was close to home, too close. The moment they arrived in Kanem the safety she'd felt for so many years dissipated to anxiousness. Changa noticed and tried to pry the reason from her but she refused to talk of it. He had his own concerns; her fears were probably unfounded. But as the days and weeks passed she relaxed. She knew her transgression had not been forgotten among her people, but at least they did not travel beyond Yorubaland, or so it seemed.

An elderly woman draped in Ihaggaren blue caught Panya's eye. She never had the opportunity to talk to the desert healers while among Warani's folk, missing the chance to increase her knowledge of healing. This woman's cart promised the opportunity to gain what she lacked.

"Hello, aunt,' Panya said respectfully.

"Hello niece," the elderly woman answered. "How can I

help you?"

"I seek healing medicines,' Panya replied.

"I have many. Are there any particular ills you seek to treat?"

"The ills are not important, only the source of the medicines. I seek those of the Ihaggaren."

The woman gave her a sly smile. "Those secrets are hard to come by."

"They are worth a great deal to me," Panya said.

"We shall see." The woman gestured for her to follow.

Panya trailed the woman down a narrow alley across the road from the main market. At the end of the alley was a merchant cart.

"The Imams frown on the remedies I sell," the woman said. "They abhor the origins but they acknowledge the necessity. Therefore I am allowed to sell my goods, but I must be discreet."

"I understand," Panya replied. "In Yorubaland it would be much different."

"So you are from the Oyo states?" the woman asked.

"Yes, but it has been a long time since I've been home."

The woman stopped then turned to face her.

"What is your name, daughter?"

Panya became wary. "Panya."

The expression on the woman's face warned her that something was wrong.

"I am sorry, Panya."

The woman pushed by Panya then scurried down the alley. Four men entered, their clothing and weapons familiar to Panya. Despair settled inside her. Her people had not forgotten.

The lead man was wide with muscular arms, brandishing a sword in each hand.

"How dare you return, oba slayer?" he shouted. "Did you think we would forget? Did you think we would stop searching for you?"

Panya dropped her basket, tossed off her robe then grabbed her whip and sword. The man's eyes drifted to the whip and he hesitated.

"What are you waiting for, Akuji?" the man behind him said. "Kill her and take her head!"

Akuji jerked his head toward his cohort. "Shut up, Dipe! I am the leader here!"

Panya took advantage of the distraction. Her whip kissed Akuji's face as he turned toward her. His hand went instinctively to the pain, which was his undoing. Panya stabbed him then jumped away as he fell forward. Dipe attacked her immediately, swinging his sword and club with energy but no skill. She cracked her whip at his chest which tore his shirt and sliced his chest. His club barely missed her head as she ducked his wild swing then cut him across the abdomen as she slipped by him.

The other men backed down the alley, their weapons drawn. Panya advanced on them just as cautious then stopped. She looked over their heads and saw others with bows and throwing spears waiting for her to emerge. She was doomed out in the open. The narrow passageway would serve as an advantage.

Her hope vanished when she heard shuffling overhead. Two men crept on the rooftops, bows and spears in hand. Panya sheathed her sword then snatched free her throwing knife. She waited until they were parallel to the men before her then threw the knife, striking the spear bearer. He yelped then tumbled from the rooftop, landing atop her attackers. Panya ran then leaped over the tangle of men. She flinched as an arrow creased her cheek. Panya charged out of the alley, cutting down the first man attempting to block her escape. She didn't take the time to assess her predicament, instead she moved like a deadly dancer, her whip striking like a viper, her sword blocking and slashing. Pain came and went as some of the attackers hit their mark but none of her wounds were serious.

"In the name of Sonni Ali, cease this madness at once!"

Panya's attackers scattered as the Songhai soldiers arrived. A few escaped; the rest corralled by Songhai lances. Panya panted as she took stock of her wounds. The commander of the soldiers emerged from the tangle of men then came directly to her. His stern face was a mix of curiosity and concern.

"Are you okay?" he asked.

"I 'm fine," she answered.

"I am Soumayla Berro, commander of the city guard. Why were these men attacking you?"

Panya managed to smile. "They were attempting to settle an old debt."

Soumayla turned to his soldiers. "Take them to the compound."

"You will come with us as well," he said to Panya. "I may have more questions."

"Send out word for a man named Changa Diop," Panya said. "He will explain everything. You will find him in the merchant district."

She followed the soldiers to the compound, a mud brick building surrounded by a thick wall occupied by Songhai soldiers patrolling the ramparts. The patrol leader shouted and the gate swung open. Panya was taken to a separate room where she had time to patch her wounds. Some of her attackers' weapons were poisoned; she was lucky that she retained some of her herbs in her dress pockets. They would not heal her but they would stave off the poisons' effects until she could reach her other medicines. She leaned against the wall, closing her eyes to rest. No sooner had she done so did she find herself standing in a black void, the air damp and cool around her.

"They did not succeed. I am thankful."

Panya did not know where she was, but there was no doubt who spoke to her.

"Momma?"

Her mother appeared before her and tears immediately

flowed from Panya's eyes. Her mother had come to her as an ancestor. She rushed to her and felt the fleeting warmth of her embrace.

"Momma! I should have come back sooner!"

"No, Panya. You came when you should."

They let each other go.

"Your father has passed on to the ancestors, as have I. Only your brother remains. He is Alaafin, but he cannot rule alone. His enemies gather around him."

Regret welled in Panya. "If only I had not been so selfish."

"It is done. You cannot go back and change your life, but you can make amends. Come home, Panya. Your brother needs you. Your people need you."

Momma faded, taking the darkness with her. When Panya opened her eyes Changa stood before her, his face tight with concern.

"Panya, what happened?" he asked.

He sat beside her then enveloped her in his strong arms.

"I was attacked," she said.

"I can see that," he replied. "Who would do this?"

"I'll explain later," she answered as she wiped her eyes. "Right now I wish to leave."

"That won't be a problem," Changa said. "Follow me."

They entered the main compound room.

"Who is the commander here?" Changa asked.

Soumayla stepped forward.

"I am," he said. "This woman said you would explain why she was fighting men in my marketplace."

The commander's eyes went to the gold ingot hanging from Changa's neck, a symbol that he was under Sonni Ali's protection.

"She is under my protection," Changa said. "I thank you for saving her. I'll be sure to express my gratitude to the sultan."

Soumayla frowned. "Allah be with you then."

"And with you," Changa replied.

Nafasi and the others waited for them outside. The young navigator rushed to Panya, his face full of concern.

"Lady Panya, are you okay?"

Panya smiled weakly, her strength sapped by the poisons. "I'm fine, Nafasi. I need to get to my herb bags."

"Why were you attacked?" Changa asked.

"I told you I'll explain everything once we reach our compound," Panya replied. "For now I must save my strength."

They mounted horses then galloped back to the compound. Panya was so weak that Changa helped her from her horse then carried her inside.

"Are you sure you can do this?" he asked.

"Yes," Panya replied. "With your help."

Nafasi brought her herb bag. Panya pointed out the necessary herbs then instructed Changa on the proportions. He grinded the herbs together then handed them to her with a gourd of water. Panya swallowed them then drank. The medicines took effect quickly; soothing energy rushed through her body.

"What else to you need?" he asked.

"Rest," Panya replied. "We will talk later."

Changa kissed her. "Don't die."

Panya grinned. "I won't. I promise."

Changa backed out of the room smiling. Panya smiled back until he left the room then grimaced. The poisons were more powerful than she assumed. It would be a rough next few days. She hoped she could keep her promise to Changa.

2

OYA'S DAUGHTER

Panya awoke three days later to a nervous audience. Changa, Nafasi and the others stood vigil about her bed, joined by another face she didn't recognize and a man dressed in the garments of an imam.

"I hope you haven't watched me the entire time I slept," she said.

"No we haven't," Changa replied. "But you were never alone."

"I thank you all," she said. "But now I need some time with Changa."

Knowing grins came to a few faces; the Imam frowned then stormed from the room.

"I'm sure your words were misinterpreted by some," he said.

Panya laughed. "It doesn't matter. Thank you for saving me."

"You saved yourself with your herbs. I just got you to them."

"I owe you an explanation," she said.

Changa shook his head. "Everyone is entitled to their secrets."

"This is more than secrets. I must tell you this before I leave."

Changa's eyes widened. "Leave? What do you mean leave?"

"I'm going home to Yorubaland."

Changa looked confused. "I thought you said you would never go back. You were quite certain of it."

Panya sighed. "I told why I left Yorubaland, but I didn't tell you the entire story."

Changa pulled up a stool then sat. "I'm listening."

"You know that I was betrothed to a man I didn't wish to marry. What you didn't know was that I killed him before I fled."

Changa leaned away. "You have a way to refuse a marriage, don't you?"

"I didn't intend to kill him," Panya explained. "Oya sat on my head that night. It was her will that he should die. I fled to a distant village, hoping my transgression would keep my family away. But it was not to be. My husband-to-be clan demanded revenge to prevent a war, so my brother was sent after me to bring back my head. He almost did."

Panya stopped talking, fighting to keep tears from coming to her eyes. That day was the worst day of her life. She never understood how Wole turned on her. She remembered the look in his eyes as he attacked her. There was no sympathy or love in them, only hate and anger.

"I fled far after that. I ran until I reached Mombasa. If I could have bought passage on a merchant dhow sailing east I would have done so. But I remained in Mombasa and set up my herb practice. The rest you know."

"So why are you going back?" Changa asked. "Why risk your life?"

"Because my mother's spirit came to me," Panya answered. "She asked me to return home and help my brother."

Changa's eyes narrowed. "You would help him after what he tried to do to you?"

"He is my brother," Panya said. "The trouble he deals with now is my doing. If I can end it my mother's spirit will be at peace. And so will mine."

"You might die trying," Changa said.

They were quiet for a long time. Changa finally stood, folding his arms across his chest.

"If you feel you must do this then so be it. When do we leave?"

"No Changa," Panya said. "This is something I must do alone."

"I forbid it!" Changa said.

Panya sat up in her bed. "You what?"

"I forbid it," he said again. "I won't lose you because of some debt you think you owe the brother that tried to kill you."

"First of all, you can't 'forbid' me to do anything!" Panya said. "Second, this is something I must do alone. The possibility that I might not return does not sit well with me, but my obligation goes beyond my own wishes. There are those I must answer to, those who deserve a better outcome if I can make it possible."

"We'll talk about this later," Changa said.

Panya watched him storm from the room. He had no intentions of letting her leave alone.

Later that night she emerged from her room. The smell of goat stew reached her nose, making her hungry and nervous.

"Lady Panya, what are you doing?"

Nafasi hurried toward her. "Changa said you were to rest all day."

"It's your fault," Panya said. "The aroma of that stew is irresistible."

"You didn't have to leave your bed," Nafasi said. "I can bring you a bowl once it's done."

"I'm here, so I can get my own bowl," she said.

Panya walked with Nafasi to the cooking pot. As he scooped out stew she added the powder she concocted hours ago. Nafasi handed her a bowl filled with the aromatic stew.

"Thank you, Nafasi," she said.

She walked back to her room. She ate slowly, listening as

the compound became quieter and quieter. When she finished her bowl she packed her belongings then emerged from the room. Everyone was unconscious. The powder would keep them so until sunrise; by that time she should be well on her way. She stopped at Changa's house before going to the stables. The Bakonga lay in his bed, a frown on his handsome face. He probably suspected something the moment he became groggy but in the end he could do nothing about it. She kissed him on the cheek.

"I'm sorry, Changa, but I must do this alone," she whispered. "I hope you understand. I hope I'll see you again."

Panya backed away until she reached the door then hurried to the stables. After saddling her horse and securing her provisions she rode through the compound, glancing from side to side at her slumbering companions. For so long they had been her family, but it was time for this part of her life to end. She was Oya's daughter, and it was time for her to return home.

3

TULA

Panya traveled as far as she could before reaching a small village on the outskirts of Gao. Not wanting to spend the night in the bush, she decided to test the hospitality the Songhai were so famous for. She spotted a solitary compound in the distance then guided her horse to it.

She approached the battered compound fence then opened it. She led her horse to the first house then knocked on the door.

"Who is it as such a late hour?" a woman called out.

"A weary traveler in search of a night's rest," Panya called back.

She heard shuffling then the door creaked open. A young woman stood before her, her tattered clothes and worn face revealing her as a person of ill means.

"Hello, sister," Panya said. "I am Panya. I seek shelter for the night. In exchange I'll share my food with you."

The suspicious woman's eyes brightened.

"Come in, sister," she said. "My name is Tula. Your company is appreciated."

Panya entered the home. There was no furniture; only a sleeping cot and a battered stool. The fireplace had not been used for quite some time.

"Where is your husband?" Panya asked.

Tula scowled. "He left to march with Sonni Ali. He said he would bring back enough gold dust to make us wealthy. Three years he's been gone."

Panya took out her food bag. There was bread and yams inside, which did not need a fire. Tula drooled by the time Panya handed a yam to her.

"Why are you here alone?" Panya asked. "You should be home with your family instead of starving alone."

Tula bit deeply into the yam then moaned. She chewed as she answered.

"I married my husband against my parents' wishes," she said. "He is a Tuareg."

Panya nodded. In her brief time in Songhai she discovered the hatred between the Songhai and the Tuareg.

"You still wait for him?" Panya asked.

"I have no choice," Tula answered.

They ate in silence. Panya felt the weight of the day on her shoulders and yawned.

"I only have one bed," Tula said. "You are happy to have it for the night."

"I will not put you out of your own bed," Panya said.

"You have given me the first food I've had in a week. Giving you my bed in return is not nearly enough."

Panya decided to take Tula's offer. No sooner had she settled into the bed did she find herself before her mother again. They gazed at each other, melancholy smiles on their faces.

"I wish I'd been there for you," Panya said.

"It was not meant to be, Panya. Our lives are woven in Olodumare's thread. We can only follow."

"Will Wole accept me?" she asked.

Her mother looked away.

"Wole is not as you remember him. The responsibilities of rule have hardened him. He is not well liked; many of our people wish to see him dead. The only thing that keeps him in power is the will of the elders. He is still the closest to the ancestors."

"How will my presence help him?" Panya asked. "I brought our people to war."

"That you did, but many of our people admire you. You stood for Oyo. Our people wish to do so as well. But your baba and brother feel an alliance is a better choice."

"They may be right," Panya said. "Our city is not as strong as Oyo."

"It could be, with the right spirit."

Panya was puzzled. "What do you mean?"

Her mother smiled. "You are Oya's daughter. She will tell you when it is time."

Panya awoke the next morning then quickly packed her things. Tula looked on, sadness in her eyes.

"I wish you safe passage on your journey," she said. "Allah be with you."

Panya looked at the woman. "You should come with me."

Tula's eyes went wide, a smile coming to her face.

"I...I have never traveled," she said. "I would be a burden to you."

"If you stay here you will starve," Panya said. "If you come with me you'll be well fed. You can keep me company and we can protect each other. Besides, I don't think your husband is coming back."

Tula glanced at Panya's weapons.

"I think you will be protecting me. But I am a good cook and I am strong."

"Then it is settled," Panya said. "Gather your things. We go to Yorubaland."

It didn't take Tula long to pack for she had little. When they approached Panya's horse the beast snorted then shuffled away. Panya grabbed the reins then pulled it close. The horse neighed then reared up on its hind legs. Tula backed away.

"I don't know what's wrong," Panya said. "It's never been so skittish."

"Maybe it is afraid of me," Tula said.

Panya looked at the frail woman and grinned. "I don't think so. But it might be best to keep your distance."

"It's okay," Tula replied. "I can walk."

They set out early, making good time every day. At night they found a discrete place to camp, either a clear field with good protective bushes or an abandoned home. The dry grasslands slowly gave way to green savannah, the flat land transforming into low hills cradling wide sluggish rivers in their verdant valleys. Panya felt her pulse race as the the Yoruba highlands emerged before her, the northernmost region of her people's land. Apprehension quickly followed; she was a wanted woman. She glanced at Tula, the small woman walking beside her horse staring ahead with no notion of the situation she was about to encounter. Panya admonished herself in silence; she let her selfishness get in the way of what was best. She stopped her horse then dismounted.

"Tula, I must speak with you," she said.

The woman came to her with innocent questioning eyes, making Panya feel that much worse.

"You should go back," she said. "This is my homeland, but it is dangerous for me. Anyone with me will be in danger as well."

"So why do you return?" Tula asked.

"Because there is something I must do, something that is more important than my safety."

Tula looked away. "It is good that you tell me this. Long ago someone I loved very much did not tell me of the danger he put me in. But you have been honest. I will stay with you."

"You don't understand," Panya said. "You could die."

Tula smiled. "I will stay with you. There is nothing for me in Songhai."

"So be it," Panya answered. "We'll travel the bush instead of roads and we can't seek shelter in any village until I reach my home city."

"I understand," Tula said. "I won't be a burden. I

promise."

The women entered Yorubaland. As Panya said they traveled the bush, avoiding any settlements. For the first three days they fed from Panya's provisions, but by the third day they were out of food. Panya searched her bags and found a few herbs and two yams.

"We must hunt," Panya said.

"I'll go," Tula replied.

She stood then walked away from the camp.

"You have no weapons," Panya called out.

"I am very quiet," Tula called back.

Tula trotted away until she disappeared into the distance. Panya shrugged then set about building a fire. As she gathered wood she found a water hole. She made sure there were no crocodiles or other predators in the vicinity before gathering the water. Tula labored by the fire when Panya returned, dressing out a young antelope. There were bruises on her arms, but otherwise she was in good health.

"You must be very stealthy," Panya commented. "And stronger than you look."

Tula looked up from her work with a smile. "I was very weak when you found me. I couldn't hunt for myself. I'm better now."

Panya joined her. They prepared a portion of the meat to eat then smoked the rest for the journey. The smoke attracted a few hyenas but Panya drove them away. After a filling meal they settled in for the night, sleeping under the expansive sky.

Panya awoke to the ground trembling under her back. She sprang to her feet, grabbing her sword and knives.

"Tula!" She looked about the camp but could not find her companion. Panya had no time to look for the woman. She had to protect herself. She mounted her horse then waited. Moments later the riders appeared, bearing torches to light their way. As they neared Panya tensed. It was the group from Gao that attacked her earlier. There were many of them; too many. She'd lingered too long to flee; she would have to make a stand. Panya took out her sword and whip then kicked her horse forward. Her confidence faltered when she saw the lead rider aiming an arrow at her horse. Dropping her whip then sheathing her sword, she tried to turn her mount but it was too late. The rider released the arrow. It streaked then sank into her horse's chest.

The arrow was surely poisoned. Panya threw herself clear of her faltering mount. As she struck the ground she heard her horse emitted an unnatural cry of pain. By the time she regained her feet the horse was dead and her attackers were bearing down on her. The bowman reloaded his bow then took aim at Panya. She was about to dive to the ground when a dark shape rose between her and her attackers. Men cried out then tumbled from their saddles as their horses reared in terror, neighing and grunting. The large object disappeared, chaos in its wake. The archer regained his feet, stalking toward Panya. He raised his bow again; Panya braced herself, preparing to try to dodge the arrow as she had seen Changa do. But the archer never released the arrow. A large serpent rose before the man; he screamed as the reptile's head struck out, sinking its teeth into his neck. The serpent flicked its head to the left, slinging the man away. Then it plunged back into the grass, barely visible as it worked its way to the confused assassins. Another man screamed as the serpent coiled around him then crushed him in seconds. Again it disappeared into the grass. The assassins ran, leaving their horses and weapons.

Panya did not move, straining her eyes as she searched the grass. She looked ahead then saw what she dreaded. The grass shifted side to side, the serpent working its way toward her. She held her sword steady, wishing she had her whip as well. The grass ceased moving. The serpent slowly emerged, its eyes meeting Panya's. Instead of the cold blank stare of a beast, she saw emotion in the serpent's eyes.

"Tula?" she whispered.

The serpent transformed before her, its body drawing in as it took the shape of the Songhai woman. Tula stood naked before her, a shy smile on her face.

"I told you I could help," she said.

Tula scampered away to retrieve her clothes while Panya watched in stunned silence. The little woman then sat before her.

"There was a drought in our land," she began. "My father possessed a very large farm; it was our wealth. Every night he called to the ancestors for rain but they did not listen to him. One day went to the local sohanci. The sohanci told him that if he made a sacrifice to Bida, the rain would return. So my father chose me to sacrifice. I was his only girl, and the sohanci told him that Bida only takes girls."

Panya face became hot with anger. She could see the same anger in Tula.

"But I fought them," she said between her teeth. "Baba and my brothers had to tie my hands and feet to take me to the lake. My brothers cried as they carried me, but my father showed no emotion. His farm was more important to him than me. When they left me on the shore I cursed him until I lost my voice. That night, as the moon rose over the lake, Bida came. It slithered from waters then rose above me. I expected it to eat me, but instead it bit me then pulled me into the water. I held my breath as long as I could. When my mouth finally opened water flowed into my lungs but I did not choke. The ropes fell away from my body as I transformed into a serpent, a daughter of Bida. For a long time afterwards I terrorized the lake shore, attacking anyone who dared approach it. I killed only those who attempted to kill me."

Tula wrapped her arms around herself. "But soon the people had enough. They summoned the most powerful sohancis in Songhai to drive me away, and they did. I hid my serpent form until I was well away from the lake, only taking the form when I needed to feed or protect myself."

"So your story about your husband leaving to fight was a lie," Panya said.

"Forgive me, Panya. I was trying to protect myself."

Panya folded her arms across her chest. "You were going to eat me."

Tula looked at Panya. "Yes. But you offered me food and kindness. It's been a long time since someone has does such a thing. So now I am your sister. I will never harm you."

Tula had come to her aid against the assassins, but Panya still harbored misgivings. Humans tainted with spiritual powers were unpredictable. She was an example.

"Thank you for sharing your story with me, Tula," she finally said. "But don't be surprised that I am wary of you."

"I will prove to you I am a woman of my word," Tula replied. "You will see."

Panya frowned. Tula came to her then touched her arms.

"I promise. You will come to trust me like a true sister."

Panya wished she could believe her.

4

HOME

A warm wind blew across the open land separating the silent city from the surrounding forest. The houses and farms surrounding the double walled metropolis were difficult to see under the crescent moon, but Panya did not need the moon's luminance. She knew this city by heart, every house, street, family and farm. This was home.

She eased back into the woods, Tula by her side. Together they returned to their campsite then sat before the waning fire.

"It is good to see your home, isn't it?" Tula asked.

"Yes it is," Panya answered. Her mind and heart churned like an ocean storm. So many memories swirled inside her, battering her resolve like a hapless dhow. But the tempest inside was comforting as well. Oya was rising, making her presence known. Panya would have to be careful.

She reached into her herb bag, dropping a few leaves into the boiling pot of water suspended over the flames. The aroma calmed her a bit; drinking the tea would soothe her even more.

"I'll go into the city tomorrow," she stated. "If I'm allowed to speak with my brother I will find out why it was so important I return."

"Why wouldn't you be allowed?" Tula asked.

"I've done things in the past that have made his life difficult."

Tula rolled her eyes. "How difficult can his life be? He's an alaafin."

"The weight of rule is not easy to bear," Panya said.

"Because of me my homeland was plunged into war. I think it's been so since I left."

"You are a good woman," Tula said. "He will see that."

"I may be now, but long ago I was selfish."

"Is it selfish to want for yourself?" Tula asked.

"For me it was."

Panya looked into her brewing pot. The water had taken on a brownish tinge, a sign the tea was ready. She grasped the handle with a folded cloth then filled her gourd. She offered the tea to Tula but she refused.

"I was a princess," Panya continued. "There are obligations that come with lineage. Mine was to marry to form an alliance. When I refused my duty it was as if I rejected the will of my family and my people."

Tula scowled. "Everyone wants to plan our lives for their benefit. We should live for ourselves."

Tula stood, her little hands balled into fists.

"You shouldn't go, Panya," she said. "You should go back to your man and your friends. Or you should go with me."

Panya sipped her tea. Calmness spread through her body and a smile came to her face.

"I ran before, Tula. I won't run now."

She looked at her new friend, impressed by her ferocity. "Tomorrow when I go into the city I want you to stay behind."

Tula's eyes widened. "Why? I'm not afraid!"

"I know you're not," Panya said. "I don't know how things will go. If they go bad I'll need you to rescue me or go for help."

"If I come you won't need to send for help," Tula answered.

"Your talent is formidable, but there are people in my homeland that could test even my abilities. No, it's best you stay behind. I will send for you if I need you."

Tula sat. "I'll do as you say. But if you don't return in two days I will come for you. "

"I'm sure you will," Panya replied.

The morning came too soon. Panya awoke groggy, the tea's calming affect lingering. She gathered her possessions then packed them on her horse. Tula watched, chewing her fingernails. After a few moments Panya was ready.

"Are you sure you don't want me to come?" Tula asked.

"I'm sure," Panya replied. She hugged Tula then mounted her horse.

"Be diligent and stay out of sight. I 'll return as soon as I can."

Panya nudged her horse into the open. They crossed the grasses to the wide road leading to the city, joining the parade of merchants, farmers and others heading into the city for the day's work. Most people did not look at her; the fact that she rode a horse identified her as a woman of means. A few dealers approached her offering their wares but she politely refused. Then there were those whose looks lingered, those old enough to remember the princess that defied her father and plunged their city into war. They whispered and pointed, increasing Panya's nervousness. By the time she approached the city walls, the crowd mostly kept their distance.

There was no doubt the guards flanking the gates recognized her. Both ran into the city when they saw her, yelling and waving their spears as they disappeared down the broad thoroughfare leading to the palace, her former home. She entered the city like a dignitary without an entourage, the city inhabitants lining the street to see her. Some looked on in wonder, others in anger. Moments later four riders galloped up to her followed by a corps of heavily armed spearmen. The lead horseman rode up to Panya and a smile came to her face. The horseman returned her smile.

"Ekundayo,' Panya said. "It has been a long time."

"Yes it has, Panya," he replied. "It is Aare Ekundayo

now."

Panya smiled "I'm impressed."

Ekundayo grinned. Panya remembered Ekundayo favoring her. He was always eager for her compliments. Some things had not changed.

"I was sent to bring you to the Alaafin," he said.

"My brother, you mean?"

Ekundayo frowned. "You are to call him by his title. He's not happy with you."

"We will see how long that lasts," Panya replied.

Ekundayo's smile faded. "Don't take this lightly, Panya. Your return proves him a liar and shakes the elders' confidence. With the death of your mother…"

Ekundayo's voice trailed off.

"I know, Ekundayo," she said. "Mama's spirit came to me. I have mourned for her."

Ekundayo nodded. "We must hurry now. It's not good to keep the Alaafin waiting."

Ekundayo turned his horse about and they trotted together to the center of the city. Panya followed as the other warriors formed ranks around her. Together they proceed to the Alaafin's compound. Thoughts of her mother and father and her good times with Oyewole caused tears that she quickly wiped away. This was no time for emotion, at least until she knew how she stood with her brother.

The palace guards stood at attention before the palace entrance. Panya dismounted then followed Ekundayo inside, the palace guards replacing her warrior escort. She was tempted to break away then run to her old room, but this was not her home anymore. It was Oyewole's palace and her status was uncertain. When they reached the entrance of the audience chamber Ekundayo turned and gave her a reassuring smile before entering. Panya followed him inside. She did not like what she saw. Oyewole sat on a gilded stool, his face hidden by strands of red beads hanging from his crown. In his right hand he held the royal whisk; his left hand rested in his lap. The elders seated on either side of her brother were not the elders she knew. None of the previous elders were old enough to have transitioned since she'd gone, which meant Oyewole had replaced them with those more favorable to his whim. They wore robes of rich fabric that fell from one shoulder, their necks decorated with gold talisman. The man standing beside her brother as Basorun angered her. His purple robe alone showed his was favored; the fact that he wielded the ebony staff crowned with the golden lion of her family removed all doubt of his status. Babarimisa was the most arrogant of Oyewole's friends and the least liked. His parents were not Yoruba; they were Fon from Benin who had fled to their homeland and begged for refuge. She always wondered why Oyewole considered him a friend. Now he was his most trusted man.

They prostrated before the Alaafin and the elders.

"Rise sister Panya, so we can look upon you. It has been a long time," Babarimisa said in his shrill voice.

"It has been a long time," Panya replied. "But it is not you I wish to speak to."

"No one speaks to the Alaafin directly," Babarimisa answered. "The boy you once called brother has been elevated by the elders and the ancestors. He is above your status."

Panya laughed. "I will accept my place among the ancestors. I will not take seriously the boys and girls in this room that choose to call themselves elders. Has Oyo sunk so low that children now guide her fate?"

"Leave us!" Oyewole said.

Babarimisa's face twisted in shock. "Alaafin! No one is permitted to..."

"I said leave us!" Oyewole shouted.

Babarimisa prostrated before the Alaafin then led the elders and others out of the chamber. Ekundayo, the last to exit, closed the door behind him.

"It is good to see you, Wole," Panya said.

"Why have you returned?" he asked.

"I missed you," Panya replied.

"You speak as if I should welcome your presence. I don't. I ask again; why are you here?"

Panya took a moment before answering. The man sitting before her was no longer her brother, her twin. He was the Alaafin of Oyo. He was also her enemy. She would have to be careful.

"I am here because mama asked me to come," Panya said. "She said you would need my help. After seeing your court, I agree."

Oyewole took off his beaded crown. "If you wanted to help me, you would have accepted your marriage. Instead you killed your husband then fled. My life has been cursed since that day."

Panya lowered her head, unable to bear Oyewole's accusing stare.

"Wole, I am so sorry," she whispered. "I couldn't stomach the idea of marriage to that beast."

"Did you have to kill him?" Oyewole shouted. "Two men died that day, your husband and our baba."

Panya jerked up her head. "You can't blame me for baba's death!"

"Can't I? We went to war because of your actions. Baba died during that war. You might as well cut him with the sword yourself. Olodumare knows you are capable of it. You almost killed me."

Panya could take no more. "Mama was wrong. I am not needed here. You wouldn't listen to me if I tried. Goodbye, Wole."

"No," Oyewole said. "You will stay. We can't change the past, but we can secure the future. And you will help me do so."

"What are you talking about?" she asked.

"I'll let you know when it is arranged," he said. "Until then consider yourself a guest of the Alaafin."

"A guest?"

Oyewole put on his crown. "Ekundayo!"

The chamber door creaked open then Ekundayo entered, prostrating before Oyewole.

"Alaafin?" he asked.

"Take Panya to the foreigner's suite. Make sure she is well protected."

Ekundayo came to his feet then gestured for Panya to follow him. Panya did not move.

"So I am to be your prisoner?"

Oyewole did not answer.

"Please follow me, Panya," Ekundayo whispered. "Please."

Panya stared at her brother a moment longer then trailed Ekundayo from the room.

"I'll speak to him," Ekundayo said. "He will change his mind."

"I doubt he will," Panya answered. "He blames me for his situation. And in a way he is right."

"What will you do?" Ekundayo asked.

"I'll do what I'm told," Panya said. "But I can't speak for Oya."

Ekundayo shook his head. "I was afraid you would say that."

5

A PAINFUL RECOVERY

Changa couldn't remember his head ever hurting so much. He strained to sit up but the pain pushed him back to his cot, his hand massaging his throbbing forehead. He was finally able to stand after his third attempt then immediately fell to the floor, the impact rendering him unconscious for another hour. The second time he came to it was to the insistent urging of Nafasi.

"Changa, Changa. Are you okay?"

Changa sat up then dusted himself off. "Of course not. How are the others?"

"Everyone in the compound suffers the same condition. I think we were poisoned," Nafasi replied

Changa rubbed his chin. "Not poisoned, drugged. Where's Panya?"

"She can't be found," Nafasi said.

Changa thought on the conversation he and Panya had earlier. "Damn it."

He struggled to his feet.

"Is anyone well enough to fetch help?" he asked.

"Yes," Nafasi answered.

"Send for a druggist," he said.

"What about Panya?" Nafasi asked.

"You won't find her," Changa said. "She's gone home."

Nafasi's face reflected his confusion.

"Do as I say," Changa said. "Now."

Nafasi hurried from his house. Changa sat hard on his bed, his anger tempered by his throbbing head. Why was she so determined to go home alone? She said the journey might be dangerous, which made it more important that he travel with her. Whatever the reason, it was important enough for her to drug them all before leaving.

The druggists arrived and began administering their concoctions to the compound. Changa paced about, grabbing men as soon as they seemed fit to help gather goods to sell at the market. He was cashing in everything they had so they could travel as light as possible. The recovery took days, thwarting Changa's plans with every minute passed. On the third day the Soumayla visited the compound. Changa greeted him in his house.

"The word in the city is that someone tried to poison all of you." The commander sat before Changa, chewing on a kola nut as he spoke.

"Poison is too harsh a word," Changa replied. "Drugged is more appropriate."

Soumayla shrugged. "Where is your woman?"

Changa smirked. "I don't know."

The commander's eyebrows rose. "Is she dead?"

"She's the one who drugged us."

Soumayla held back a laugh. "You should have left her in my custody."

"She is a good friend, just confused," Changa said. "Soumayla, I need a guide who can take us to Yorubaland."

The commander rubbed his chin. "There are a few that travel the region frequently."

"I'll pay well for their services."

Soumayla stood to leave. "I'll send someone soon."

He strode to the entrance then stopped.

"Your woman," he said. "Isn't she from Yorubaland?"

"Yes," Changa replied.

"Maybe you should leave her there."

"She would prefer that, but that's not going to happen," Changa said. "I deserve an explanation and I'm going to get it."

Changa and his men were ready to travel after three more days of recovery. Changa managed to work the markets to his favor, trading his bulky items for those easy to carry. The commander's man finally arrived, wrapped in colorful robes with a full beard covering his face. Changa, engrossed in counting his profits, did not look up as the man bowed before him.

"I hear you are in need of a guide to Yorubaland," the man said.

Changa looked up. "Yes I am. Are you that man?"

The man bowed again. "I am Shekarau Audu of Hausaland. I am at your service."

Changa stood then shook the man's hand. "You know the way?"

"I do. Where in Yorubaland do you wish to go?"

Changa frowned. "I'm not sure."

Shekarau pulled at his beard. "That could be a problem. The Yoruba are a city folk and very quarrelsome. It would help to know which city you seek."

"I know where we can find out," Changa replied. "Come with me."

They mounted their horses then road to the Songhai military compound. Changa found Soumayla in his office.

"Do you still hold the men who attacked Panya?" he asked.

"Only one," the commander replied. "We exiled the others but this one refused to leave. He says they will be executed for failure if he returns home."

"Take me to him," Changa said.

The commander took Changa and Shekarau to the holding cells. The assassin had been well kept despite his crime. Changa was tempted to stab him, but his information was important.

"What is your name?" he asked.

"Nasiru."

"The woman you were sent to kill is a good friend of

mine, a very good friend."

Nasiru drew away from Changa.

"Don't worry; I won't hurt you...yet. I need to know where she is from."

"Oyo," the man replied.

Changa looked at Shekarau.

"I know Oyo. It is the largest city-state in Yorubaland."

"Then that is where we go," Changa said.

6

REVENGE

Panya walked through the royal compound flanked by a score of Oyo guards. It had become her routine of late and it unnerved her. She had no idea what her brother planned for her, but the signs were not good. Her messages to him had been refused and she had not been allowed her herbs. He probably feared she would find a way to us them to escape.

The guards escorted her back to her room as the sun descended below the compound walls. The sounds of the city ebbed, its inhabitants settling in for the humid night. Panya languished in her large room, her head propped up with her hands. The knock on her door was unexpected yet welcomed.

"Who is it?" she asked.

"Ekundayo."

Panya opened the door. The young Aare entered with a smile.

"Forgive me for disturbing you so late," he said.

"No, I'm happy for the company," Panya replied. "Ekundayo, what is Wole planning for me?

Ekundayo's smile faded. He sat on the floor, crossing his legs then folding his arms on his lap.

"Oyo is in a dire state," he said.

"When has it not been?" Panya replied.

"This is more serious, Panya. Since your mother's death Nupe and Borgu pressure us from both sides. They are demanding tribute that we cannot provide and our armies are not strong enough to fight two wars. We must seek an alliance."

"And I am the seal," she said.

"Ogundipe, Nupe's Oba, is interested in you," Ekundayo said.

"Who sent the men to Songhai to kill me?" Panya asked.

"They were probably sent by Ladipo, Borgu's Oba," Ekundayo answered. "He fears an alliance between Oyo and Nupe."

"How did they know I was there?" she asked.

"The Borgu have strong juju," Ekundayo said. "Ige, their sorceress is equal to your mother. It is suspected that she is the cause of your mother's death."

Panya's back straightened. Ekundayo's words struck her like a physical blow.

"My mother was murdered?"

Ekundayo nodded. "Her health failed rapidly after a diplomatic visit from the Borgu. It was not poison, for everyone shared the same food during the meetings. Ige was part of the Borgu delegation. She spent the most time with you mother. When your mother fell ill she was immediately suspected."

"And what did Oyewole do?" Panya asked.

"Nothing," Ekundayo answered.

Panya felt Oya's rage surge through her, her hands trembling.

"You must understand, Panya," Ekundayo said. "We're not children anymore. We must control our reactions. We must weigh each decision and consider its consequences. We are in a delicate situation."

"Don't talk to me as if I was a child," Panya said. "A sorceress comes into our city, accepts our hospitality, kills our mother and Oyewole does nothing for the sake of diplomacy?"

"It shows his control," Ekundayo said.

"It shows his weakness," Panya replied.

Panya paced the floor. Why did her mother not tell her? She appeared only to tell her of Wole's troubles and nothing of her own demise? She stopped pacing as a sick thought came to her mind. Could it be what she saw was not her mother? Was it an image planted in her head to lure her to the same fate?

"I must go," Panya said.

"Oyewole won't allow it," Ekundayo said.

Panya struck Ekundayo on the temple, knocking him unconscious.

Panya took Ekundayo's sword. She didn't want to kill anyone, but she would if necessary. She peeked from her room. The hall was curiously empty for the moment; she moved quickly to the room across the hall where her belongings were stored. When she stepped back into the hallway she was greeted by a familiar large serpent.

"Tula!"

Tula slowly transformed to her human form. She smiled innocently.

"I told you I would come," she said.

Panya grabbed her hand then dragged her back into the other room. She found a dress for the woman. It sagged around her but it would have to do.

"Come with me," Panya said.

Together they slipped through the palace, avoiding the fearful inhabitants that dared travel the hallways. The word had spread that a giant serpent was on the loose. Members of the royal family hid in their rooms, while palace guards that were supposed to hunt down the mystical intruder were invisible. They hid as well, fearful of the magic that they assumed summoned the large beast.

Panya and Tula were halfway across the compound courtyard before they were challenged. A group of guards strode toward them, their bodies covered with kapok, their hands gripping swords and shields.

"You must return to the palace!" the lead warrior shouted. "There is a serpent about!"

Tula needed no prompting. The dress fell into a pile by Panya; moments later Tula the serpent emerged. The warriors yelled then ran.

Panya scooped up Tula's dress then followed her serpent sister out of the compound. They hurried through the city, using the alleyways between compound walls to hide their escape. Once they reached the forest they rested. Tula regained her human form then dressed.

"I'm glad you came," Panya said. "My escape would have been more interesting without you."

"Your brother was not happy with you?" Tula said.

"No," Panya said. Her mind drifted to other matters.

"My mother was murdered, Tula," Panya said.

Tula gasped, her hand covering her mouth.

"I must kill her killer. Will you help me?"

"Of course," Tula replied.

Panya knew the way to Borgu. As a young girl they were educated about the surrounding obanates. Borgu and Nupe were considered Oyo's greatest threats, so it was important that they knew all about them. The duo travelled in secret at they had before, staying away from major roads and making camp in the brush. Once they crossed into the lands claimed by Borgu they restricted their travel to night only. Borgu most likely sent the assassins after her; they would be hunting her still. As they traveled deeper into Borgu certainty settled into Panya as the reason for her return crystalized in her mind. It was unexpected, but there was no doubt of what she must do.

Borgu was a sparsely populated land unlike Yorubaland. The Borgu preferred small villages to the clusters of cities populating Panya's homeland, so it was easy to travel without being noticed. Her destination was Illo, a city on the banks of the Niger. It was the oldest city of Borgu and its spiritual center. If Ekundayo was right Ige was a person of great power and would most likely reside in this city. A slight breeze caressed her skin as the thoughts passed through her mind. Oya was with her.

Panya and Tula camped that night outside the outskirts of the city. Tula brought fish from a nearby river and a small antelope which they cooked then ate with relish. Panya looked upon the city as she ate, her mind focused on the task ahead. Tula cleared her throat to get Panya's attention.

"What is it, sister?" Panya asked.

Tula smiled. "You called me sister. I like that. I didn't have a sister, only brothers."

Panya returned her smile. "Neither did I. It was only me and Wole. And now it seems I don't have him."

Panya put down her bowl. "We've been through much in this short time together, more than most siblings experience in their entire lives. If we are not sisters, what else could we be?"

Tula's face became serious. "Then as your sister, I ask you not to go into Illo."

Panya returned Tula's serious countenance. "You know why we are here. I have to. "

"No you don't." Tula took her hands. "I know your mother's death is heavy on your heart, but what good would your death serve? We could leave like you did before. We could travel until we find a place where we can live in peace. You say Sofala is a good place so let's go there. I have never been so far away."

Panya shook her head. "I wish it was that easy, Tula. I left Oyo running away from my destiny. I know now what I need to do. My travels prepared me for what is about to happen. Oya is with me. I can feel it."

"I don't trust the spirits," Tula replied angrily. "You see what they have done to me."

"Bida saved you by transforming you," Panya replied. "Be mindful of it."

Tula looked away. "Still, I would rather be dead sometimes."

Panya touched the young woman's shoulders. "But you're

not. You are here with me. We are sisters and I'm glad of it."

Tula touched her hand then smiled. "I am, too."

Panya's expression became serious. "I would tell you to stay here, but I know you won't. So stay close to me and don't do anything stupid. This sorceress won't be impressed or frightened by your ability. She will have her own help."

Tula nodded.

"And if I tell you to go, you go," Panya said.

Tula's eyes narrowed.

"Promise me," Panya said.

Tula looked down. "I promise."

Panya knew Tula lied, but getting her to make a promise would at least force her to consider escaping if Ige proved stronger than she suspected.

"Let's go," Panya said.

Together they crept through the darkness toward the city, staying close to the hedgerows dividing the farms surrounding the small city. The mud walls were low enough for them to climb. Illo was typical of most Sahelian cities, walled family compounds separated by narrow alleys bordering wide avenues leading to the center of the city and the compound of the oba. Panya's attention was immediately drawn to a compound to the right of the oba's lair, its walls decorated with talisman and spiritual images. The energy emitted from the compound assured her that this was her destination. She took her sword in her right hand; her whip in her left, and then proceeded to the compound of her mother's killer.

A few feet away from the compound she knew she was expected. The feeling of anticipation swept over her as a breeze stirred around her.

"Oya is with us," she said, more to soothe herself than to inform Tula. The compound gate stood open and unguarded, an ominous invitation to her.

"It's time we meet, murderer," she said. Panya faced Tula.

"Stay here."

Tula's nodded then backed into a nearby alley. Panya crept toward the open gate.

A wave of nausea struck her as soon as she entered the compound. She dropped her weapons as she fell to her knees clutching her stomach. Women dressed in white dresses emerged from the temple marching single file, red beads hanging from their necks. They circled Panya, chanting a song she could not recognized but she knew held dark intentions. The nausea increased, forcing her to spew out the contents of her stomach. Weakness coursed through her. She collapsed into the dirt.

She felt her head lifted then looked into a foul wooden mask.

"You knew what waited for you, yet still you came," a woman's deep voice said through the mask. "You are braver than your brother. Not much smarter, but much braver."

The woman turned Panya onto her back. She was tall, possessing a frame resembling that of a male warrior. She wore a leather skirt festooned with gris-gris, her upper body draped with beaded necklaces. The sorceress took off the mask then smiled, revealing bright sharpened teeth.

"Ige," Panya managed to say.

"You contain much strength inside you," Ige said. "I must have it. Your mother escaped my grasp. She was too strong for me to claim it, and she would not walk into a trap."

"Oya will protect me," Panya managed to say.

"Oya has no power here," Ige spat back.

A strong wind howled through the compound, pushing the Ige onto her back. She sprang back to her feet.

"Chant louder!" Ige shouted at her cohorts. "Oya comes!"

The women chanted louder, then screamed. Panya's captor growled.

"What is...by the ancestors!"

Tula the serpent loomed over the sorceress, swaying from side to side. Panya felt the nausea subside. She rolled over, lifting from the ground with one hand while searching her pouch for a poultice that would counter Ige's juju.

While the acolytes were terrified by Tula, Ige was unmoved. She took a dagger from her belt then grabbed a handful of black powder from a bag tied about her hips.

"You are no dragon, little girl," she hissed.

Tula hesitated, and then continued to sway. The woman grinned.

"Yes, I see inside you," Ige said. "You've been Bida blessed, saved by his bite. But you don't possess his strength, or his protection!"

Ige threw the black power then spit into it. The power exploded into dark clouds that swallowed Tula's serpent head. Tula let out a mangled scream as she flailed away from the woman.

Panya swallowed the poultice. It took effect immediately, clearing her head as it firmed her stomach. She grabbed her whip and sword then charged toward Ige who was raising her dagger, about to strike a killing blow to Tula. Panya cracked her whip around the woman's hand then yanked back, spinning her around. Ige gripped the whip with her free hand then yanked Panya to her. Ige opened her left hand; a column of white smoke rose from her palm then transformed into a sword. She sliced the whip in half.

Ige pounced on Panya with sword and dagger. Panya parried as she backed away, struggling to match the woman's speed while recovering from the effects of her magic. A slice across her shoulder cleared her mind. She blocked a downward strike then punched out, striking Ige in the face. The blow had an exaggerated effect, knocking the sorcerer from her feet. She slammed against the ground, sliding to the compound wall. Panya ran at Ige, rage pulsing throughout her. Overhead dark clouds formed as a stiff wind blew through the city. Panya smiled; Oya was with her.

Ige was kneeling when Panya ran up to her then drove her knee into her face. Her zealousness almost cost her life; Ige managed to swing out with her blade as she fell backwards, barely missing Panya's throat. Rain fell as the women circled each other, both bleeding from dozens of wounds.

"It doesn't matter if you kill me," Ige said. "Your mother will still be dead. Fate has been set into motion. As long as your brother rules there is no future for Oyo!"

Panya rushed the sorceress again. Ige stabbed out weakly; Panya knocked her blades aside then drove her sword into the woman's chest. A dozen lightning bolts struck the ground around them, followed by deafening thunder.

"My work is done," Ige whispered. She fell against Panya then died.

Panya shoved the dead woman to the ground. There was no satisfaction in taking her life, just the feeling of a duty that had to be done. The rain became a torrent, a blinding downpour to everyone except Panya. Oya was here protecting her.

"Panya! Panya!"

Panya followed Tula's voice and found her lying in the mud, bleeding from a wound in her side. She picked up the woman, cradling her.

"Come sister," she cooed. "We're done here."

Panya strode from the compound with Tula in her arms, sheltered by Oya's drenching rain. Around her chaos swirled, panic voices reaching her ears. But only one sound rang in her ears, the dying words of Ige.

"As long as your brother rules there is no future for Oyo."

7

Ambush in Borgu

Changa twisted hard in his saddle to avoid the saber aimed for his throat. He sprang back, stabbing his attacker through the ribs. The man tumbled from his mount as Changa yanked the reins of his horse to confront the two riders coming at him from behind. He took quick stock of their situation. The baharia held, but they were hard pressed. He cursed his bad judgment in allowing Ekundayo to lead them to Yorubaland instead of Shekarau. In exchange for his freedom the man led them into a trap. Ekundayo lay dead on the side of the road; one of Changa's throwing knives in the back of his skull.

Changa pushed his mount to the nearest rider. Their swords sparked as they met, the other man almost losing his weapon from the force of Changa's blow. The second strike shattered the blade, sending iron shards into his eyes. Changa cut his throat then turned in time to bock a stab from the other rider. This man proved to be a better swordsman but no more lucky. Changa's sword found his gut and the man doubled over against his horse's neck. The horse spun away, guided aimlessly by its dying rider.

A roar of voices caught Changa's attention from behind. He turned his mount to see baharia and Borgu fleeing side by side in terror when only moments ago they were after each other's blood. An involuntary shudder passed through him, warning of what approached. He dismounted his jittery steed then sheathed his sword. The blade would be no use in this fight; the terrified animal a hindrance. Only the throwing knives forged in the fires of Kongo could aid him now.

The tebo careened down the road, bellowing a sickening cry. The creature took the form of a misshapen vifaru, with two horned heads protruding from an elongated neck. Changa shifted from foot to foot as he tried to determine how to approach the monstrosity. Although she could not help him, he missed Panya, if only for her encouragement. The baharia, not even Nafasi, could overcome their fear of Changa's constant nemesis. He would fight the beast alone, hoping that the ancestors were not ready for him to sit with them.

He ran toward the beast, a knife in each hand. Both heads lowered, their horns aimed at him. Changa threw the first knife at the head to the left. The beast swung the head right, knocking the knife away and exposing its neck. Changa threw the second knife at the juncture of the heads. The blade hit its mark and both heads bellowed in pain. The beast increased its pace and Changa sprinted to his right, seeking safety among a stand of trees. The vifaru followed, slamming its heads against the thin trees and rattling its horns between them. Changa faced the trapped brute, taunting it by waving his hands. It pushed its heads deeper into the trees, grunting with effort. Changa worked his way around the beast then hurried into the open again. The vifaru tried to follow him but could not. Its heads were tangled in the trees.

Changa knew he had only moments before the beast freed itself. He ran to its hulking body then climbed onto its back with his knives. The beast howled then jerked violently to free its heads to no avail. Changa raised his knives then plunged them into the neck juncture. The beast shuddered then let out a deafening squeal. With a massive jerk it freed its heads then bucked Changa from its back. He hit the ground then bounced and rolled his way back to the woods. From the cover of the bush he watched the tebo flail about, trying in vain to remove the knives. Its breathing came hard as it slackened then stopped. With a shudder and strained cry it fell to its knees then tumbled to its side.

Changa emerged from the woods as did his baharia. Shekarau joined his side as they all watched the tebo die then melt away into a putrid mass.

"What sort of devilment is this, Changa?" Shekarau said, disgust heavy in his voice.

"A familiar one," Changa replied.

The Hausa merchant glared at Changa. "You are a cursed infidel. I shouldn't have come with you."

"But you did, and you've been paid," Changa replied. He rested his hand on the hilt of his sword.

"I was wrong to trust Ekundayo, but you still know the way to Oyo and you will lead us there."

Shekarau snatched his purse from his belt then threw it down at Changa's feet.

"I break our contract! I will not travel with a cursed infidel!"

Changa's sword was out its sheath, the point digging into Shekarau's neck.

"I don't have the time or patience for this. You will take us to Oyo. Once we arrive you can go where you wish. Now pick up that gold dust and get on your horse. Try to escape and you'll find a blade, or a knife or an arrow in your back. Do you understand me?"

Shekarau glared at Changa then went to his horse. Nafasi came to Changa.

"The Borgu have fled. We suffered no deaths, only a few wounded."

"Good," Changa replied. "We ride on to Oyo."

Changa mounted his horse and the men gathered around him.

"God will punish you for this, Changa Diop," Shekarau shouted.

"Maybe so, but not today," he replied.

Shekarau glared at Changa a moment longer before he

spoke again.

"We can't go through Borgu," he finally said. "There may be more assassins waiting to stop us."

"Then what do you suggest?" Changa asked.

"We head west. We can go around Borgu then approach through Sabe."

Changa rubbed his grizzled chin. "How much time will that add to our journey?"

"A week, maybe two," Shekarau replied. "It is a mountainous region and a journey I don't prefer, but in times of war one does what one must do."

Changa had no qualms fighting his way through Borgu, but he had to make the best decision for his men. Panya might be in trouble, or she might be welcomed home in glory. It was a hard decision to make, but he had no choice. He was no use to Panya dead.

"Then we will go through Sabe," he said.

8

THE NEW ALAAFIN

Panya knelt over Tula, cleaning the snake woman's wound then applying fresh poultice. The concoction would eventually draw the poison from her veins but it would take time. Ige's magic was much strong than Panya expected, especially against someone like Tula. She cursed herself for not preparing the young woman properly for the battle. She should have made her gris-gris, but she assumed Tula's bond with Bida would protect her. She was wrong.

Once Tula was settled she tended to her own wounds. Her gris-gris protected her from the worst, but she didn't escape completely. Her energy drained quickly, leaving her almost breathless after a few hours. So she slept most of the day, waking only to eat, relieve herself, and tend to Tula.

The rumble of distant thunder caught her attention. If she strained she could see the storm still raging over Illo, keeping the city under siege as she made her slow escape. It was another sign that Oya was with her.

After two days of travel they happened upon a small village near the border of Oyo. A sorghum farmer offered them a place to sleep for the night which they eagerly accepted. Tula was stronger now, staying awake longer and eating more. That night, as Panya sat before an open fire cleaning her weapons Tula came then sat beside her.

"Thank you for saving me, sister," she said.

"You should be scolding me," Panya replied. "I didn't protect you properly. If I had, your wounds would not have been so severe."

"Maybe so, but I'm still alive because of you."
Tula hugged Panya's neck, surprising her. Panya smiled then leaned her head against Tula's as she grasped her forearm.

"What will you do now since you have avenged your mother?" Tula asked.

"I'm going back to Oyo," Panya answered.
Panya felt Tula stiffen then pull away from her.

"I understand now," the young woman said.

Panya turned to face her. "Understand what?"

Tula's expression was serious. "You wish to die."

"Of course not!" Panya said.

"You returned to your home knowing your brother hates you. You go alone to find the woman who killed your mother. Now you will go back to your brother after escaping to give him another chance to kill you. You wish to die."

Panya looked away. "It seems like that, doesn't it?"

Tula placed a gentle hand on her shoulder. "I understand. When Bida first took me I felt the same way. I was no longer a woman; I was a monster. I could never fall in love and marry. I would never have children or grandchildren. My life was over, so why prolong it? So I attacked anyone that came to the lake, hoping that one day there would be enough men and enough spears to bring my death. But there never was. And then the people stopped coming to the lake. They would rather die of thirst than face me."

"If you really wished to die, why did you fight them?" Panya asked.

"Because I wanted them to die with me," Tula replied.

"If you had died we would never have become sisters," Panya said. Her words brought a smile to Tula's face.

"This is not about me. It is about you. Why do you wish to die?"

"I don't," Panya answered. "Even though I don't fear it.

When I came back to Oyo I was uncertain why. But with every step my purpose has revealed itself. I now know why I am here, why I have returned. I must see it through."

"I see," Tula replied.

"This is not your fight, sister," Panya said. "You can leave whenever you like and I won't think any less of you."

Tula shook her head hard. "I will not leave you, Panya. You have treated me with more love and kindness than anyone I've ever known. I don't agree with you returning to Oyo, but I will go with you."

Panya was half hoping Tula would leave. It was possible Wole would try to have her killed, but he would not succeed. Not as long as Oya stood with her. But she couldn't be sure Oya would extend her benevolence to Tula. Panya took a deep breath then resumed cleaning her weapons.

"I'm happy you are with me," Panya said. "Now go back inside and get some rest. Tomorrow we set out for Oyo. We'll need all our strength."

Tula kissed her cheek then returned to the house. Panya oiled her sword as a warm breeze cradled her like a mother's embrace.

"Yes Oya," she whispered. "Tomorrow will be the beginning of many great things. I hope I survive them."

After another week of travel they arrived at Oyo. Panya and Tula waited until dark as they did before, sneaking into the city unknown and unnoticed. This time they did not travel to the palace. Instead their destination was a group of homes forming a semi-circle to the right of the palace.

"Where are we going, sister?" Tula asked.

"These are the homes of the rightful elders," Panya said. "There is one I need to speak to."

It was hard to find the home in the darkness, but Panya eventually discerned the mamba totem beside the ebony wood door. She knocked on the door then waited.

"It is too late for visitors," a woman's voice answered.

"Go away!"

"There was a time when it was never too late for Amoke," Panya replied.

The door flew open. A woman with graying hair and a chubby face looked at Panya and Tula with wide eyes.

"Panya!" the woman exclaimed. "Quick! Come in!"

The woman dragged Panya into the house then hugged her tight.

"I am so happy to see you alive!"

"Thank you, Adenike," Panya answered.

"Wole said you escaped the palace," Adenike said. "He said he didn't know if you were alive or dead and he didn't care."

"Wole is a different person from what I once knew."

Adenike finally noticed Tula.

"Who is your friend?" she asked.

"I am Tula, aunt."

Adenike hugged Tula as well.

"Come with me," she said. "Baba will want to speak to you."

"I was hoping he would," Panya said.

They followed Adenike through the public room then into the private quarters. Omope sat on his favorite stool, working a kola nut between his jaws. He read a scroll, his eyes transfixed on the document.

"Baba, Panya is here," Adenike said.

Omope's head jerked up. A wide smile came to his face as his eyes glistened. He dropped the scroll then rushed to Panya, wrapping her in a hug.

"My niece lives!" he said. "She lives!"

Panya hugged him tight, feeling safe for the first time since she ventured to Oyo. Omope was her father's brother and his closest friend. While her father's position as Alaafin forced him to be stern with her and Wole, uncle Omope shared the love baba could not. He was also a powerful elder; the perfect person to help her carry out her plan.

"So," he finally said. "Why have you come to me now? You should have come as soon as you returned."

"I'm sorry, uncle. Momma's spirit came to me and urged me to help Wole. I didn't know what type of help he would need so I went to him first. I thought time had softened his opinion of me, but I was wrong."

"Wole doesn't hate you, Panya," Omope said. "If anything he envies you. You fled Yorubaland and he could not. He had to shoulder the responsibility of his duties alone. It was a struggle for him to become Alaafin, a very hard struggle."

Panya read the meaning of Omope's words. "You don't approve of him."

Omope looked away. "The position of Alaafin is not inherited as you know. There are those who are closer to the ancestors than Wole. One sits before me."

Panya nodded her head. It should have been obvious the day Oya chose to sit on her head, but she denied it. It was the reason she fled Yorubaland. She understood that now.
"If given the choice the Oyo Mesi would not have chosen him," Omope said.

"I wasn't ready then, uncle," she said.

"Are you ready now?" Omope asked.

"I think so," she said.

"Do not think, Panya. We are about to play a dangerous game. I must be sure you are ready to take the stool."
Panya closed her eyes, silently asking for Oya's word. A slight breeze brushed her face, warm and comforting.

She opened her eyes. "Yes, uncle. I am ready."

Her uncle smiled. "Now that that is settled we must deal with another issue. As you know I am no longer consider an elder, nor are the others who rightfully hold the lineage. Wole has replaced us with children."

"How could he have done so?" Panya asked.

"Ekundayo," Omope replied. "He will not march his army against our outside enemies, but he is quick to use it against anyone challenging Wole's word."

"He will listen to me," Panya said.

Omope's look became stern. "Don't confuse boyhood infatuation with love, Panya. You have no idea how ruthless Ekundayo can be."

"I will have to try. He's been nice to me so far," she said.

"Uncle, please gather the true elders and make ready."

Omope nodded.

"Uncle, I need to ask another question. Where can I find Ekundayo?"

"He has a farm outside the walls, close to the river. He goes there at sundown."

"Then there is still time," Panya said.

"You are going tonight?" Omope asked.

"Time is essential," Panya said. "War is coming to Oyo and we must prepare."

Omope looked skeptical. "How do you know this?"

"Because I started it," Panya replied.

Omope dropped his head in his hands. "With who?"

"The Borgu," Panya answered. There was no remorse in her voice. "I went to Ile and killed Ige."

"Then you are right. We must see Ekundayo tonight."

Panya raised her hand. "No uncle, stay here. Tula and I will go."

"I know who sits on your head," Omope replied. "But what of this girl?"

Panya smiled. "She is Bida blessed."

She noticed a flash of fear cross Omope's face. "How you would find one such as this is beyond me. It is another sign that you are meant to sit on the stool."

Omope walked with them to the entrance, hugging both

women before opening the door.

"Be careful, Panya," he said.

"I will, Uncle," she answered.

Panya and Tula worked their way out of the city then into the countryside. Ekundayo's farm laid a few miles away, the crescent moon high overhead when they arrived. It was late, too late to call on anyone, but Panya was determined to bring things to order as soon as possible.

"Stay outside, Tula," she said. "I may need you to rescue me."

"I'm ready," Tula said. "I will be close."

Panya marched across the open expanse to the house, well aware of the guards watching her approach. They seemed unconcerned; apparently a woman visiting Ekundayo in the middle of the night was a common occurrence. The thought made her angry and anxious. Ekundayo might think more of her visit than intended. She would have to be firm with her words.

She reached the gate. It was unlocked and unguarded so she pushed it open then proceeded to his home. His guards barely acknowledged her. In fact, they looked way, avoiding her eyes. It was their way to be discrete in case a woman appeared with child and claimed Ekundayo was the father, she assumed. By the time she reached his door she was furious. It reflected in how she pounded it with her fist.

"Who is it?" Ekundayo said angrily.

"An old friend," Panya replied.

"I made no arrangements for tonight! Do you..."

Ekundayo snatched the door open and the words he was about to utter stuck in his throat.

"Panya?" He grabbed her arm then snatched her inside. "What are you doing? Have you lost your mind?"

"I need your help," she said, ignoring his confusion.

"Wole is searching all over for you!" Ekundayo said. "If he finds you here he will think I was involved in your disappearance."

"Are you really worried, Ekundayo?" she asked. "How can my brother's enforcer fear him?"

A smile came to Ekundayo's face. "I could take you to him and be rewarded."

"Would you do that, Ekundayo?" Panya asked.

"Of course not. You know how I feel about you. As long as you stay with me you'll be safe."

"I have no intentions of staying with you," Panya said.

"I'm here for your help. I want to re-install the true elders. Once they are in their rightful place they will choose me as the new Alaafin. When that is done we will go to war against Borgu."

Ekundayo looked at her wide eyed then burst out laughing. "You? Alaafin?

"You see humor in this?" Panya asked. "Are you so blinded by your selfishness that you cannot see Wole is killing our people?"

Ekundayo raised his fist to strike Panya but a gust of wind lifted him off his feet then flung him across the room, slamming him into the wall. He tried to rise but the wind pinned him to the wall.

Panya sauntered to him. "My husband tried to strike me and I killed him. I don't need you as an enemy, Ekundayo. Nor do I need you dead. I need you as an ally."

Ekundayo struggled against Oya's grip. "What do you promise me, Panya?"

"You will remain Aare, but you will fulfill your duty and fight our enemies, not our own people," she said.

Ekundayo smiled. "So be it."

Panya waved her hand and Oya released Ekundayo. He stood, straightening his robes.

"Come with me," she ordered.

Panya turned then walked away. She didn't concern

herself with any retaliation by Ekundayo. Each situation steeled her confidence and confirmed her decision. As soon as she and Ekundayo stepped into the compound courtyard he began shouting orders, gathering him men around them. Tula appeared as they left the farm, a stern look on her face. Panya smiled.

"It is alright, sister," Panya said. "They are with us."

Tula and Ekundayo exchanged suspicious looks.

A crowd gathered at Omope's compound, a mixture of elders, their followers and the curious awakened by the commotion. Panya, Tula and Ekundayo approached Omope.

"So you are with us, Ekundayo?" Omope asked, his eyes narrowed.

"I am with Panya," he replied.

Omope nodded. "I guess that is enough for now."

Ekundayo turned to Panya. "I and my men will lead you. Wole's guards will not let us through. They are sworn to protect the Alaafin."

"Then I shall lead us," she replied.

"No!" Ekundayo reached out to her then dropped his hands. "They may harm you."

"His guards are most likely my relatives," Panya said. "We will see where their loyalties will fall. But stay close."

Ekundayo nodded. "I will."

Ekundayo's men cleared the way for Panya and the elders. The crowd marched to the palace in silence, the tapping of their sandaled feet the only sound. Panya kept a stern face while inside she shook like a child. She knew Oya was with her but she could not predict the action of her brother. If she was challenged she had no idea what Oya would do. She did not want to harm Wole, but she could not control an orisha, especially one as powerful as Oya.

Shouts rose from the palace compound as the crowd neared. Guards appeared on the ramparts, shields, spears and bows in hand. The gate opened and more guards flowed from inside, forming lines on each side of the gate and blocking the entrance. One guard stepped forward, a burly man swathed in leather armor who towered over the others. He held a war club in one hand; the other hand resting on his sword hilt.

"What is the meaning of this?" he shouted. "What are you people doing here?"

Ekundayo took the lead, walking before Panya with both hands raised.

"Stand aside, Keffi," he said. "The elders have come to meet with our Alaafin."

Keffi studied the group, his eyebrows rising slightly as he recognized Panya. His fingers tightened on his sword hilt.

Ekundayo approached the man. "Think carefully about what you do next, my friend. The wind is changing in Oyo. Make sure you are on the right side."

"It is my duty to protect the Alaafin," Keffi said, his voice unsure. "You also know it is forbidden for warriors to enter the palace."

"The new Alaafin stands before you," Ekundayo answered. "Why would I be with her otherwise?"

Keffi cut a glance at Panya again before turning to face his men.

"Open the gate!" he shouted."

Ekundayo patted the man's shoulder. "A wise decision, my friend."

"I hope so," Keffi replied. He snatched out his sword then stabbed Ekundayo. Panya watched stunned as Keffi pulled the sword free then came at her.

"Oyewole is my Alaafin!" he shouted.

He stabbed at Panya. The sword pointed at her heart turned away, ripping her shirt. Tula held Keffi's arm, struggling with all her might to keep him at bay. He clubbed her with his free hand, sending the woman sprawling to the ground.

Panya snatched her whip free then cracked it across Keffi's

face. He winced as the beaded leather plowed a blooded row across his forehead. She cracked the whip again, cutting his cheek. Keffi backed away, turned then ran for the palace. The guards on the ramparts released their arrows and threw their spears, showering death onto the startled crowd. A ring of warriors surrounded Panya, Tula and Ekundayo, shielding them from the lethal downpour. Other warriors pushed the elders to safety among the surrounding compound walls. Panya fumbled with Ekundayo's robe, searching for his wound. What she found did not bode well for the Aare.

"You need help," she said.

Ekundayo shoved her hand away. "You need to get into the palace."

Ekundayo raised his arms and his warriors helped him to his feet.

"Warriors, clear those ramparts!" he shouted. "Take the gate!"

Oyo warriors formed pods of protective shields for his archers, who released their arrows on the ramparts. The palace guard tried to hold positions but the warriors' barrage was too heavy and too accurate. They abandoned their position, leaving the dead and wounded behind. As the archers cleared the heights other warriors advanced on the gates.

"Go with them," Ekundayo said. "This is what you wanted."

"Not like this," Panya said.

"It wasn't your choice," Ekundayo said. His legs buckled then he collapsed in the street.

"Take him to a healer," Panya said, surprised at the authority in her voice. Three warriors responded, one warrior picking up the Aare while the others protected them with their shields. The other warriors gathered around Panya and Tula.

"Let's move!" Panya shouted.

They ran toward the gate in formation, spears lowered. The

guards waited, shouting curses and insults at their natural rivals. Shields crashed together and the warriors fought. Panya jumped into the midst of the melee, cracking her whip and swinging her sword, her body fueled by Oya's presence. The guards fought hard, but they were vastly outnumbered. They faltered, giving way to the warriors. Panya took position before the warriors then led the way through the palace, pausing only to take a look at Keffi's body before proceeding. They met no resistance in the corridor leading to Wole's audience chamber. Apparently her brother had concentrated all his efforts on keeping them outside the palace walls.

A group of warriors surged before Panya as they reached the closed doors of the chamber. They burst through, the doors slamming against the mud brick walls. Warriors spread out along the wall, spears lowered. Panya and Tula entered to see Wole sitting on his stool, flanked by his elders. Wole faced looked tired as he managed a smile.

"You have returned," he said.

Panya strode to her brother, emotions roiling inside her head. She knew this was the right thing to do, but sympathy toward her brother would not go away. A small part of her did not agree with her actions.

"I know what I must do, Wole. I know why mamma called me home."

Wole tilted his head, a sad expression on his face. "So this is how you help me?"

"Oyo suffers under your rule," she said. "We pay tribute to nations who should yield to us. You use our warriors to punish our own people. You surround yourself with sycophants, not people of wisdom. This is not what the ancestors want of us. It is not what they expect from you."

"These are your words," he replied. "Do the elders feel the same?"

Omope stepped forward, joined by the other elders.

"We do," he said.

"Then who am I to disagree?" Wole extracted a knife from his robe. The warriors surged toward him until they realized the knife was meant for him. Panya grabbed his hand before he could finish.

"No!" she said.

Wole gazed at her with pained eyes. "You know this is tradition."

Panya looked at Omope. He nodded his head in agreement with Wole.

"No I said." Panya pried the knife from Wole's hand.

Panya turned to the onlookers. "He is my only family. I will not have him die. If he does you must choose another Alaafin."

The elders gathered together, their voices low and urgent. Omope finally stepped forward, a disapproving look on his face.

"Already you instigate change," he said. "But it is done. Wole can live, but he must go into exile."

Panya turned to her brother. "Do you accept the decision of the elders?"

A look of relief flushed his face. "I do."

Omope and two elders stepped forward. Wole closed his eyes as they removed the Alaafin's cap from his head, and then took off the gilded robe. Wole and his elders rose from their stools in unison then filed from the chamber. Wole was the last to leave; he halted before his sister, weariness on his face.

"This is as it should be," he said. "I never wished to be Alaafin. It was a duty I accepted. You, however, are suited for it. Your mind has always been clear, and Oya sits upon your head. Be well, sister. Don't forget me."

Panya's eyes glistened as she hugged Wole. "We will see each other again, Wole. I promise."

The look on her brother's face revealed he did not believe her. He nodded then followed his elders out of the chamber.

Omope came to her.

"Panya, please take the Stool," he announced.

Panya glanced at Tula then sat on the stool. The elders draped the robe upon her shoulders, its weight symbolic of the responsibility she accepted. Omope approached with the crown, and then hesitated. He looked at Tula with a smile then handed the crown to her.

Tula's grin matched the brilliance of the rising sun as she placed it on Panya's head. No sooner had she done so did the entire room prostrated before Panya.

"Behold our new Alaafin!" Omope announced. "The elders have chosen the one closest to the ancestors, and the ancestors have accepted our choice."

The audience rose to their feet. There was no joy in Panya's heart, but neither was she solemn. It was meant to be, a destiny determined the day she called to Oya for guidance.

"What is your first command, Alaafin?' Omope asked.

Panya gazed across the room, finding Ekundayo near the entrance. Two warriors supported him between them. His wound had been treated. He stared at her, barely nodding his head.

"Prepare for war," she answered.

9

SABE

Changa cursed as he fled with his men for the safety of the nearby rocks. Stones rained down on them from the peaks looming above, thrown by warriors hiding among the crevices. He was beginning to believe this journey was cursed. Someone or something was determined to keep him from Panya, which made him just as determined to get to her.

"Damn you, Shekarau!" Changa shouted. "You did this on purpose!"

The Hausa merchant cowered beside him, holding up his tied hands.

"Believe me Changa; this is not of my doing! I know Sabe as a peaceful land. The only reason we avoid it is because of the mountains."

"Does this look peaceful to you?" Changa dared to peak from behind the boulder acting as refuge for him and three other baharia. The men pummeling them we not well armored; their weapons seemed ill made. But they were deadly with the slings they wound over their heads, releasing the rock with deadly accuracy. Three baharia lay in the road dead, their skulls cracked by the granite projectiles.

"Baharia! Don your armor!" Changa shouted. "It's time we cleared these hills of these vermin!"

A cheer rose from his men. They sprinted in unison to their pack horses, daring the rock barrage to retrieve their bundles then running back to cover. Changa put on his chain mail and helmet.

"Nafasi!" he shouted. "Organize the archers. We'll move under their cover!"

"Adamu! Zamayoni! Bashiri! Tata! Take up your bows!" Nafasi called out. "Release on my signal!"

"The rest of you will follow me!" Changa shouted.

Changa watched as Nafasi loaded his crossbow then took aim.

"Release!" he shouted.

The archers sprang up then released their arrows. Painful cries filled the air.

"Attack!" Changa shouted. He jumped from behind cover then ran uphill. The bowmen released another volley, keeping the slingers pinned down. A rock bounced off Changa's helmet, breaking his rhythm. He recovered in time to see three mountain men bearing down on him, war clubs and swords raised. The club man reached Changa first, growling as he raised his club. Changa waited until the man was almost upon him before dropping to his knees. He rammed his shoulder into the man's gut then stood. The man flipped over Changa's shoulder then slammed into the rocks. Changa shifted to his right, dodging the next mountain man's sword thrust then backhanded him on the side of the head. As the man collapsed unconscious Changa met the third man. The man hesitated; Changa did not. He stabbed the man in the gut then continued running uphill.

With the slingers pinned down by the bowmen, Changa and his men cut through the unarmored mountain men like scythes through sorghum. The mountain warriors scattered, disappearing among the higher rocks. Changa raised his hand and the baharia halted their charge up hill.

"We've broken them," Changa said. "Let's…"

Changa spotted the boulder sway from left to right before it tumbled down the hill. He loped to his right and the boulder careened by him, shaking the ground beneath his feet. The baharia scattered in every direction as more boulders rolled down the hill after them.

"Enough of this!" Changa said.

He bounded upward, dodging the man-made avalanche with the dexterity of a mountain goat. The warriors attacked again, emboldened at the sight of a solitary warrior climbing the hill. They fell on Changa en masse then immediately regretted their decision. Changa unleashed his full fury, becoming a twisting blur among warriors whose spirit did not match their skill. They faltered, running away in all directions, some even running toward the baharia. Changa's men let them pass. They were not here to win a battle; they simply wanted to get to Yorubaland.

Changa came down the hill like an angry bull, glaring at Shekarau. The merchant leapt to his feet then ran. Changa took a throwing knife from his belt then threw it at the fleeing merchant. The handle, not the blades, struck Shekarau's head and sent him sprawling. Changa stomped to the man then lifted him off his feet by his throat.

"Give me a good reason not to kill now!" Changa said.

Shekarau couldn't speak, so tight was Changa's grip on his throat. Changa threw the man to the road. Shekarau coughed then rubbed his neck before answering.

"I didn't know this would happen!" Shekarau said.

Changa kicked the man onto his back.

"You had no idea? None at all?"

Shekarau hesitated. Changa pulled his sword.

"No, Changa!" Nafasi shouted. "He is the only person that can lead us out of this land."

Changa sheathed his sword. "You are right, brother."

He snatched the merchant from the ground.

"Bring him a horse," Changa ordered.

Changa went to his fallen brothers as Nafasi secured Shekarau a horse. He knelt beside them then shook his head in frustration.

"Ramadhani, Nyabera and Lutu," he whispered. "Forgive

me, brothers. You should have been home with your families. This was not meant to be."

The other baharia gathered around him to pay their respects as well. Afterwards they buried their friends, covering the graves with rocks.

Shekarau waited on his horse. Nafasi tied the man to his saddle and held the reins. Changa walked up to the merchant.

"You'll ride point for the rest of our journey," Changa said. "If you lead us into any further danger you'll be the first to suffer."

"And what will you do to me if we make it to Oyo? Will you kill me? It is best that I die now."

"If you lead us through you'll be free to go," Changa said.

"You have my word."

"Your word means nothing to me," Shekarau spat.

Changa looked at Nafasi. "Kill him."

Nafasi drew his sword and Shekarau raised his tied hands.

"No, wait!" he cried. "I will lead you to Yorubaland. Safely."

Changa mounted his horse. "Let's hope so. Remember, any more ambushes and you'll be the first to die."

Shekarau nodded. "This woman must mean a great deal to you."

Changa managed a smile. "She does."

He snapped his horse's reins and the beast trotted by Shekarau.

"Now shut up and get us out of here."

10

WAR

The Borgu emissary galloped into Oyo on a bright morning flanked by a contingent of lance bearing warriors, their tall green turbans swaying with the rhythm of their steeds. Their arrival had been anticipated; the gates of the palace compound stood open, guarded by archers on the wide ramparts. A group of solemn servants waited at the palace entrance, immediately taking the reins of the horses as their riders dismounted. The emissary and the others strode for the entrance but were stopped by ten palace guards.

"Only the emissary can enter," the commander of the guards announced. The Borgu warriors reached for their swords.

"I ask you to take a look at the ramparts before you make any rash decisions," the commander cautioned.

The emissary snapped his head about. The archers were all turned toward the compound, their bows loaded and aimed at the Borgu. When the emissary turned back the commander greeted him with a smile.

"Follow me," he said. "The Alaafin waits."

The emissary strode through the palace flanked by palace guards. They entered the council room; Panya sat on the royal stool draped in a red beaded cloak, her face obscured by a string of crimson beads hanging from her cowry crown. The elders flanked her, their faces solemn. Tula stood closest to Panya, clothed in a white cotton dress trimmed with gold stitching. She nodded to the emissary.

"Welcome, Tatau Alkali," Tula said with a hospitable

voice. "Alaafin Panya is honored by your presence."

Tatau sneered. "There is no need for pleasantries. I've been insulted at every turn since entering Oyo. The final insult was forcing me to leave my guard outside the palace."

"A necessary precaution," Tula replied. "Seeing as though you have managed to kill our Alaafin's mother and father you can understand her safeguards."

"Where is the boy?" he said, referring to Wole.

"He is where he should be," Tula replied.

"It's a pity," Tatau said. "He was much more reasonable… and respectful."

"The ancestors no longer favor him," Tula responded.

"You know why I'm here," he said.

Tula smiled. "I would not be so forward to presume your intentions."

"The tribute!" Tatau snapped. "We did not receive your annual tribute."

Tula did not answer. The emissary scanned the room as if seeking a response from someone of higher authority. There was none.

"You play a dangerous game, Panya," he warned. "You were not here when the Borgu marched on Oyo. The rest of you were. I ask you to give this girl fair warning."

Tula was about to respond but Panya raised her hand. She stood then approached Tatau.

"True, I was not here," she said. "But I was in Illo weeks ago, so you know what I am capable of."

"Your witch tricks won't stop an army," Tatau retorted. "The Borgu is a swarm of iron. You will feel its sting."

"Send your swarm," Panya replied. "Then prepare your mourning clothes. Our sorghum will grow strong on the bodies of your warriors."

"Then there is nothing left to say is it?" Tatau said.

Panya turned her back on the emissary then returned to

her stool. Tatau shared a menacing glare then stormed from the council room, the palace guard following.

The elders dropped their rigid postures, immediately mumbling among themselves. Ekundayo came before Panya. He groaned as he prostrated before her, still suffering from his wound during the palace coup.

"So we are at war," he said.

Panya took off her crown then handed it to Tula. "We are."

Omopo came forward as well. "We still have time to send the tribute."

"No," Panya answered.

Omopo frowned. "You are as eager to fight as your brother was eager not to."

"Oyo was weak under Wole," Panya said. "And I am not eager to fight. I'm eager to restore our strength. I'm eager to stop our people becoming Borgu slaves and subsist off partial harvest while Borgu and their cattle grow fat. I have no wish to conquer them. I only wish for us to keep what is ours."

She turned her attention to Ekundayo. "Are the warriors ready?"

"Yes," he replied. "But there is a problem. We will have no cavalry. The nobles will not ride without Wole."

"Then we will march without them," Panya said.

"That is not a wise decision," Ekundayo replied. "Without cavalry we won't be able to prevent the Borgu from outflanking us. We'll also be susceptible to a charge. A few of our warriors are blooded but many are not. They may not hold up to a cavalry charge."

"We don't have a choice, Ekundayo," Panya answered. "Besides, I've learned much from my travels. We will deal with the Borgu riders when the time comes. How soon do we march?"

Ekundayo seemed to study her before answering. "Tonight if you wish, Alaafin."

"First light is soon enough. The Borgu expect us to wait for their attack. We will show them different," Panya said. "We march in the morning."

*   *   *

The hazy sunrise brought with it warriors from the ends of Oyo, from villages of only a few families to cities almost as large as Oyo. They gathered outside the city walls, chanting their local songs accompanied by a cacophony of rhythms. And contrary to their threat, the nobles came. They arrived in unison, unlike the pods of warriors that trickled in throughout the morning. The warriors gave way as the horse riders moved to the center of the celebration, stabbing their lances into the sky. The crowd became obscured by a dust storm of its own making.

Panya stepped away from the tower window. Ekundayo looked at her with an angry frown, his hands on his hips. A warrior stood beside him holding a red kapok suit. Tula stood beside him, her small frame swallowed by her blue woven armor.

"You must wear this," Ekundayo urged. "The Borgu archers have the strongest poisons. A scratch could kill you."

"I have my protection here," Panya said. She patted her herb bag dangling from her waist belt. "Besides, I can't fight in that thing. It's too bulky."

"You won't be fighting," Ekundayo said.

"Then I won't need it," she said.

Ekundayo sighed. "Leave it then. We must go. If we stay any longer our warriors will start fighting each other. Local rivalries die hard."

Ekundayo led the way down the corridor then out of the palace. The citizens of Oyo lined the street as they mounted their horses then galloped down the main avenue to the city gate. It had been so long since Oyo went to war that no one knew how to respond. Some people waved and cheered while others looked on with fearful eyes. As they rode through the gate a joyous roar burst from the warriors. The horsemen broke through the throng, riding directly to Panya and the others. Ekundayo's warriors formed a ring about her and Tula, forcing the horsemen to pull short.

"Pompous bastards," Ekundayo said.

One rider approached, a man who sat tall in his ornate saddle covered in tan kapok trimmed in red. His mount was draped in the same colors, as was the men and horses following him. He held a towering lance with double blades, gris-gris and talisman twisted tight about the shaft. The warriors arranged their horses side by side then dismounted in unison. They prostrated before her then their leader rose.

"Alaafin Panya. I am Olumoroti, son of Tiju-Iku. The riders of Iwaro have come to serve Oyo!" he bellowed. The Iwaro horsemen shot to their feet.

Tula rode forward. "We thank you, Olumoroti. The Alaafin was told the riders would not come."

Olumoroti looked at Ekundayo and sneered. "No doubt you heard such lies from the footman. We are the pride of Oyo. There can be no victory without us."

Panya urged her horse forward. "We are glad you have come, Olumoroti."

"I am Moroti to you, my oba. It is my hope that my lance will serve you well."

The double meaning of Olumoroti's words was clear.

"One war at a time," Panya answered.

Moroti laughed. "May the Iwaro lead us to victory, my Alaafin?"

"You may," Panya replied.

Ekundayo cut his eyes at Panya. He reached for the royal whisk tucked in his belt then extracted it slowly. He extended it toward Moroti with much ceremony. The rider snatched it from his hand then held it high for his men to see. They cheered as they shook their lances. Together they mounted their horses then galloped to the main road, Moroti waving the royal whisk.

The Oyo army formed a loose formation behind the cavalrymen and the march to Borgu began. Panya looked upon the army and was swept with a sudden wave of loneliness and apprehension. This was not the first time she marched off to battle but it was the first time she'd marched without Changa and the baharia. She looked at Ekundayo, her childhood friend now fearless Aare, at Moroti and his pride filled kapok covered cavalry, and at Tula, her sister of circumstance and suffering. There was no doubt in her mind that they all would fight, but as much as she tried she found no confidence in them. If it was not for Oya's presence she would turn back to the palace. She knew she would not feel this way if Changa was with her. She did not need his protection despite the fact that he would try to do so; she needed his skills, his strength, his intelligence and his love. But that was not to be. In truth it was possible she would never see him again.

"Sister, where are you?" Tula asked, her sweet voice breaking Panya's thoughts.

"I am beside you, sister," Panya replied.

"No, you are somewhere else," Tula answered. "Your city marches to war, yet you are not here. You must be here, sister. Your warriors must know you are with them and that you believe they can win."

Panya grinned at Tula's perception. "And since when did someone so young gain so much wisdom?"

"Bida speaks through me sometimes," Tula said. "He has shared his life with me, and sometimes his wisdom."

"I will be here when the time comes," Panya said.

The army marched for five days, their destination the traditional battlefield where all disputes between Oyo and Borgu were settled. The wide grassland rested beneath the shadow of two steep hills opposite of each other, a slow river flowing equidistant from each hill. Panya and the others stayed just within the trees crowning their hill, trying to spy if the Borgu army did the same.

"The Borgu must still be on the march," Panya said.

"They will be here soon," Ekundayo replied.

"How can they?" Moroti said. "We refused the tribute the day before their emissary departed. I'm sure he has not reached Illo by now.

"The Borgu knew we would refuse their demands," Ekundayo said. "Their army probably embarked the day after the emissary. They will be here soon."

"They are already here," Tula said as she pointed to the opposite hill.

Two Borgu horsemen emerged from the trees, meandering down to the river's edge. They were soon followed by scores more, the riders spreading out along the river but none of them attempting to cross.

Moroti lifted his lance. "The time for glory is at hand! Riders, follow me!"

"Wait!" Panya shouted.

The cavalry surged into the open, ignoring Panya's command. The Borgu riders galloped away from the river as the rest of their brethren emerged, joining them midway from the tree line. They wheeled then returned to the river's edge, reaching the muddy banks in unison with the Oyo horsemen.

"Call them back!" Panya said. "We must attack in formation!"

"No," Ekundayo replied. "We may win this battle with this confrontation. Besides, they wouldn't listen to me. This is tradition."

"What sort of tradition is this?" Panya said.

"You should know this, Panya. These are warriors of honor and lineage," Ekundayo replied. "If our horsemen prove themselves superior to the Borgu the Borgu will most likely withdraw. If the outcome proves otherwise the Borgu might commit their infantry. But that would not be wise."

"Our infantry is superior?" Panya asked.

"Borgu's infantry is mostly conscripts and farmers," Ekundayo said. "I made it my mission to maintain a standing army, a professional army. If they attack, we will smash them."

The clash of steel took their attention. Individual duels broke out among the horsemen on both sides of the river's edge as the warriors fought for reputation. Moroti demonstrated himself more than a boaster, felling two Borgu horsemen quickly with his blade. The other duels diminished as Moroti continued to prevail against his foes, the Borgu retreating to their side of the river as the Oyo cheered on their champion.

"Is there no one else?" Moroti shouted. "Are the Borgu like grass under the bull's hooves? Have you shed your horns and become cows?"

A roar rose from the west. Panya and the others looked in the direction of the sound. Ekundayo's eyes widened as a second army crested the hill.

"This can't be!" he said.

These warriors were not Borgu. They were covered from shoulders to feet in white tunics gathered at the waist with thick leather belts from which their swords hung. Each man carried a wooden shield with a metal circle in the center, the shield tall and wide enough to hide the entire body. Their lances were half the size of the cavalry, with the blade tips almost half the size of the lance.

"Nupe," Ekundayo said. "This is why Borgu was so anxious to fight. They knew the Nupe would come to their aid."

"Call the cavalry back," Panya ordered. "March the infantry to the hill slope!"

"What are you doing?" Ekundayo shouted. "I am Aare."

Panya glared at Ekundayo. "Then what do you suggest?"

"We'll advance to the field then form ranks with cavalry

on each flank."

"If we do so their line will be longer than ours. They could flank us on either side."

She waited for Ekundayo's shocked look to pass before she spoke again.

"If we pull back then form ranks at an angle, we'll force their right flank to climb, which we'll slow them down. We can concentrate our strength on the left then flank them."

Ekundayo strode his warriors, shouting orders. They formed the line as Panya suggested. The signal drummers called the cavalry back; Ekundayo signaled them to take the left flank. His orders were followed none too soon; the Nupe and Borgu formed ranks then advanced.

Panya turned to Tula. "Stay here with the others,' she urged.

Tula shook her head. "I will go with you, sister."

The combined army crossed the river, their war chants mingled in a steady pace. The Oyo warriors responded, jostling with each other in anticipation. Ekundayo and his officers paced back and forth, yelling at the men to keep formation.

"Follow me," Panya said to Tula. "And stay close."

She handed Tula a sword. Tula's confidence face faded to fear.

"Hopefully you won't have to use it," Panya said.

She reached the front lines just at the Borgu released their arrows.

"Down!" Ekundayo shouted. He pushed her to the ground as her bodyguards covered her with their shields. The arrows rattled against the shields; some of the bodyguards shouted then collapsed beside them. Panya's instincts took over. She rushed to them, administering antidotes from her herb bag. Ekundayo grabbed her arm then pulled her away.

"You are the Alaafin now," he scolded her. "We have healers for that. What are you doing here?"

"I came to fight," she answered.

Ekundayo looked at the advancing warriors. "I don't have time for this. Stay with your bodyguards!"

Ekundayo took his place before the warriors, ignoring the arrows falling about him and bouncing off his kapok. He raised his whisk then dropped it sharply. Oyo archers released their arrows as the spear throwers stepped through the ranks, flinging their spears at the exposed midsections of the Borgu and Nupe. Their first ranks buckled almost in unison as the Oyo volley found its mark. Despite the withering barrage the Borgu and Nupe advanced rapidly because of their sheer numbers. But it was what developed on the right flank that caught Panya's eye. The attackers compensated for the difference by running up the hill with the aid of the cavalry.

Panya broke from her bodyguards then remounted her horse. She kicked the mount into a full gallop, arriving at the end of the line moments before the first Nupe warrior. She snatched her whip from her belt then cracked it into the face of the warrior, sending him reeling back in pain. Panya worked her horse back and forth cracking the whip to break the advance. Her bodyguards arrived soon afterwards, adding their fury to her skills.

Her horse shuddered then fell. Panya threw herself wide, landing hard on the ground but away from horse's crushing weight. A lance protruded from the dying horse's throat. She scrambled to her feet in time to meet the horde of warriors eager to take the Alaafin's life. She wielded her sword and whip into a deadly frenzy, holding off the crushing press. Despite her furious skill Panya knew it was only a matter of time before she and the others were overwhelmed.

"Is this what you brought me here to do?" she said to Oya as she fought. "Am I to be the ruin of Oyo?"

Oya answered with thunder. Panya dared to take her eye off the onslaught and saw dark clouds fill the sky. A tight wind blasted down around her, knocking away the encroaching warriors then lifting her off her feet. She rose higher and higher until she saw the entire battle beneath her. The cavalry held the right flank and the left flank held because of her intervention. But the center crumbled, overwhelmed by Borgu's unskilled but numerous warriors. Oya's power surged through every inch of her body, causing her to tremble.

"Take what is yours, daughter!" Oya commanded.

Panya stretched out her hand toward the failing center and lightening burst from her fingers. Her ears filled with thunder as the bolts struck Borgu warriors, killing them instantly. Panya continued throwing bolts with both hands, decimating the Borgu center. She turned on the right flank, blasting the Borgu cavalry from their horses then sending them fleeing in panic. The left flank crumbled without her attention, Nupe warriors dropping their shields and weapons to speed their retreat. The Oyo army pursued them to the river then halted, waving their weapons in victory.

Panya slowly settled to the field in Oya's hands. Once her feet touched the grass a wave of fatigue swept over her. She fell but did not touch the ground. Ekundayo and Tula held her. Tula smiled at her; Ekundayo's face was filled with wonder and fear.

"You are truly Oya's daughter," Tula said.

"And Oyo's Alaafin," Ekundayo added.

Panya managed to smile.

"Take me home," she whispered. "Take me home to Oyo."

11

A SPECIAL REUNION

Changa and the baharia galloped into Oyo after a hard ride of three weeks through the mountains of Sabe. On the way they waded through Borgu warriors fleeing in every direction. It was an army so beaten it ignored the baharia and their wealthy caravan. The fact that Oyo was victorious did not calm his worries. Panya could be anywhere; she might be safe in the city or a captive in Borgu. She could also be dead, but he would not allow himself to consider that option.

They rode through the gates of Oyo then down the main avenue of the city, ignoring the curses and stares of the folks whom they pushed aside. Their destination was the central market. Changa knew by experience that he would find answers there. He halted his horse before the grandest stand in the market then dismounted. It was a kola nut stand worked by a woman in a bright yellow dress and towering head wrap. She looked at Changa with a frown.

"No one needs kola nuts so much as to raise such a fuss," she snapped.

"I apologize for my rudeness," Changa replied. "But I am seeking someone of great importance. Do you know of a woman named Panya? Has she come to this city?"

The woman's demeanor changed. She eyed Changa up and down as she rubbed her chin.

"And from which city do you hail?" she asked.

"I am from Sofala," Changa replied.

"Sofala? I've never heard of it. Definitely not a Yoruba

city," the woman said. "But I'm not surprised. Suitors are coming from as far as Nubia to woo our new Alaafin."

Changa was puzzled. "Alaafin? What is an Alaafin?"

"The Alaafin is our ruler," the woman replied.

Changa's eye went wide. "Panya is Oyo's ruler?"

"Yes," the woman replied. "Chosen by the elders and orishas."

Nafasi came to Changa. "What is going on?"

Changa smiled. "It seems that Panya has undergone a change in status."

"Aunt, I seek an audience with Alaafin Panya," Changa said. "How would I go about such a thing?"

"Ah, you are a lucky man," the woman replied. "I am a woman of great influence. I can arrange what you seek."

Changa read the look in the woman's eyes. The negotiations were about to begin. He had no idea she could do what she said but he had to start somewhere.

"Nafasi, bring me the chest," he ordered.

Nafasi trotted away then returned with Sonni Ali's chest. The sight of the trunk alone caused the woman to smile. Changa opened the chest, extracting two small bags of gold dust.

"Is this sufficient for your help?"

The woman snatched the bags then opened them. She smiled greedily
. "Very much so!"

She immediately shut down her stall.

"I am Tolulope Adedeji. The man I'm taking you to meet is a very powerful elder. If he cannot arrange an audience for you no one can."

She began walking then stopped.

"Bring that with you," she said, pointing at the chest. "We may need more of what's inside."

Changa and the others followed Tolulope through the market then to the center of the city. She led them to a group of family compounds, stopping at the opulent gate of the largest compound. She knocked hard and a servant appeared.

"What do you want, Lope?" the servant asked.

"This is Changa from Sofala," she said. "He seeks an audience with the Alaafin."

"My master has no time for your foolishness!" the servant said.

Tolulope nodded toward Changa; Nafasi opened the chest and Changa took out a bag of gold dust. He extended to the servant.

"For your trouble," he said.

The man opened his hand then Changa dropped the bag in his palm. The servant closed his hand like a snare.

"I will return shortly," he said.

The servant scampered away then returned, swinging the gate wide.

"You may enter."

Tolulope, Changa and the others followed the servant to a large opulently dressed man sitting on a stool under a large shade tree. The man looked past Tolulope to Changa.

"My master, Omopo," the servant said.

Omopo studied Changa with narrowed eyes.

"She said you would come," he said.

"Then you know why I am here," Changa replied.

"And why should I arrange this audience? Alaafin Panya is the best thing ever to happen to Oyo. She defeated the Borgu and the Nupe simultaneously. They now pay us tribute. She is chosen by the elders and the ancestors. Most of all, she is favored by Oya."

"I will not leave until I see her," Changa said.

"I know," Omopo replied. "Promise me you will not encourage her to leave and I will arrange the meeting."

"What Panya decides to do is up to her," Changa answered.

Omopo stared at Changa for a moment before answering.

"I will send my servant to the palace," he said.

"Thank you," Changa replied.

Omopo answered with a shrug.

Omopo provided food and drink for Changa and his men while they waited. It was nearly sundown when the servant returned, accompanied by the Alaafin's warriors. They were led by a man who scrutinized Changa like a potential rival before approaching him.

"I am Ekundayo, Aare of Oyo. I have come to escort you to the Alaafin's palace."

"Thank you," Changa replied.

"Do not thank me, foreigner," Ekundayo snapped. "I do so only to get this over with then send you on your way."

Changa didn't reply. The Oyo were not happy to see him. He began to wonder if Panya would feel the same.

They walked to the palace. Ekundayo handed Changa and his men over to the palace guard who took them through the doors and down the corridor to the audience chamber. Changa didn't realized how much he missed Panya until he saw her sitting on the royal stool, her face hidden by her beaded crown. A young woman stood beside her, a knowing smile on her face.

"Welcome, Changa Diop of Sofala," the woman said. "Our Alaafin is pleased to gaze upon your presence once again. It has been too long."

Changa was amused by the formality. "It has indeed. I am honored that the Alaafin has given up her precious time to see me."

The woman studied Changa, her eyes inspecting every inch of him.

"Now that you stand before us I can see why the Alaafin was anxious to see you."

"Tula!" Panya said.

Tula giggled then regained her formal air.

"The Alaafin wishes to speak with Changa alone."

Ekundayo stepped forward. "Is that wise, Alaafin?"

"Leave us," Panya said.

Tula shared a smile with Changa as she led the others out of the chamber. Ekundayo was the last to leave. His eyes darted between the two, his look despondent. He was about to say something when Tula returned, taking his hand then pulling him away. She closed the door.

Panya leaped from the stool, threw her crown aside then fell on Changa with kisses. Changa wrapped his arms around her, his body shaking with joy.

"I had no idea where you were!" he said.

"I'm sorry, Changa. I should have told you," Panya replied.

They kissed again before Panya took his hand then led him to her stool. She sat and he sat beside her.

"So you are Alaafin now," Changa said. "How did this all happen?"

Panya told Changa everything. As she spoke, a bad feeling settled into him. By the time she finished his feelings were clear in his face.

"So you will not go to Kongo with me," he stated.

"No," Panya answered.

Changa waited before he spoke again for he did not want to hear the response to his next statement.

"And you will not marry me," he said.

Panya looked away. "No, not yet."

"Then all is settled then," Changa said. He stood to leave.

Panya grabbed his hand.

"Wait, Changa. When I was one with Oya I saw all. I saw you, Changa, and I saw your destiny. If we were to marry you would never return to Kongo and you would never be truly happy. If I was to go with you I would be abandoning my duty."

"You saw this?" Changa asked.

"Yes," Panya replied.

Changa sat hard. "You have never been wrong, Panya, although now I wish you were."

Panya came to him, wrapping her arms around him.

"Stay with me until you are ready,' she said. "As long as it takes. But you must go."

Changa held her tight. "Yes. I must."

*   *   *

The men pushed the dhow over the launching logs into the surf. It was a small boat, sturdy enough to handle the strongest winds but compact enough for one man to manage. Changa looked at the small ship then back to Panya. He was a fool to leave her, but his destiny was miles away. She came to him and they kissed, the passion of the past three weeks stirring between them.

"I will come back for you," he said.

"We will see," Panya replied.

Changa walked away from her then stopped.

"I will come back for you."

He walked to the dhow. The baharia surrounded him, shaking his hands, patting his back and hugging him. The last to come to him was Nafasi.

"Take our brothers home, Nafasi," Changa said. "There is enough gold for all of you to live like sultans."

"Thank you, Changa," Nafasi said. "Sofala will not be the same without you."

They hugged like brothers, patting each other hard on the back. Changa grabbed his provisions then tossed them into the dhow. He climbed inside then the baharia let go of the rope. The tide and the wind pushed him into the ocean, a gentle breeze nudging him toward the horizon.

Panya and Tula remained on the beach long after the others. Panya caressed her belly, sure of the life growing inside. Tula stood beside her, placing her hand there as well.

"It will be a strong child worthy of its parents," she said. "Bida knows."

"Oya knows, too," Panya replied.

"Goodbye, Changa," she whispered. "Come back to me. Come back to us."

Together they watched until the dhow's lone sail disappeared below the horizon.

-END-

SAFARI GLOSSARY

Aare - supreme general of Oyo

Alaafin - ruler of Oyo, a powerful city-state in Yorubaland

Bwana - sir (Swahili)

Basorum - prime minister of Oyo

Kanem/Bornu - an empire that existed in modern Chad and Nigeria. It was known to the Arabian geographers as the Kanem Empire from the 9th century AD onward and lasted as the independent kingdom of Bornu until 1900. At its height it encompassed an area covering not only much of Chad, but also parts of modern southern Libya, eastern Niger, northeastern Nigeria and northern Cameroon.

Borgu - a region in western Nigeria and in the northern Republic of Benin. According to the Kisra legend known all over Borgu, the petty kingdoms of the country were founded by Kisra, a hero who according to an oral tradition immigrated from Birnin Kisra ("the town of Kisra") in Arabia. His brothers are said to have been the founders of the kingdoms of Illo, Bussa and Nikki. Other descendants are believed to have constituted the ruling aristocracy of the Wasangari.

Fahali - bull

Kibwana - 'little man'

Mai - King

Malkia - queen

Mbogo - buffalo

Mtwana - slave

Nupe - a loose confederation of towns along the Niger in the 15th century.

Oyo - a Yoruba empire of what is today western and northern Nigeria. Established in the 14th century, the Oyo Empire grew to become one of the largest West African states.

Sohanci - sorcerer

Polepole mtu - slow one

Ugali - is a dish of maize flour (cornmeal) cooked with water to a porridge- or dough-like consistency. It is the most common staple starch featured in the local cuisines of the eastern African Great Lakes region and Southern Africa.

Coming in 2015,
the final journey of Changa Diop
Son of Mfumu
By Milton J. Davis

Mombasa. Sofala. Indonesia. The Middle Kingdom. Vijayanagar. Yemen. Ethiopia. Kanem/Bornu. Songhai. Oyo. Home.

Changa's safari has taken him to the ends of the earth, seeking the means to return to his home and claim the land stolen from his father. He returns alone, hoping to fulfill a promise made as a boy. But Kongo has changed radically since Changa's escape. Different powerful factions fight for control, include those from far away. At the center of the turmoil is Usenge, manipulating the players for his own ends. And he has prepared a special reception for the boy who is now a man…

The feeble flame pricked the thick blackness, a fruitless effort against an overpowering void. A man sat before the anemic fire, his muscled upper body bare except for the intricate tattoos etched into his umber skin. A leather loincloth draped over his waist, resting on his thick crossed legs. His face was unknown; a wooden mask concealed the features. He swayed to a rhythm unheard, his breathing in time with his side to side motions. To one observing he seemed in a trance. But such was not the case.

The foliage about him trembled but the motion and sound did not break his state. Three shapes entered the light; beings resembling the mysterious primates inhabiting the densely forested hills. One look into their hard faces and gleaming eyes revealed a different presence indeed.

The Ndoki sat side by side opposite the swaying man, their eyes locked on him. The man swayed for a few more moments then ceased.

"What have you seen, Usenge?" they asked in unison.

Usenge, the masked sorcerer, ruler of the Kongo, peered at his cohorts through the eye slits of his permanent mask.

"The son of Mfumu has returned," he said. His voice was deep and ancient like the river meandering near them.

"What of the tebos?" they asked.

"They have failed," Usenge said.

"Then it was meant to be."

Usenge nodded.

The Ndoki stood together. "Will you be ready?"

Usenge stood before his brothers. "I will."

The Ndoki disappeared into the bush. Usenge eyes lingered where they once stood. They would not help him as they did with Mfumu. He was alone in this fight. He shrugged his shoulders. It did not matter. He was much stronger now. He would not fail. Changa Diop would die.

He stomped the fire with his bare foot, extinguishing the flame. The darkness rushed upon him like a lover long denied and he took comfort in its embrace.

9 780996 016711